CRAB & SNAIL

The TIDAL POOL of COOL

For Jake & Matt—B.F.

For Carter and Randi—J.C.

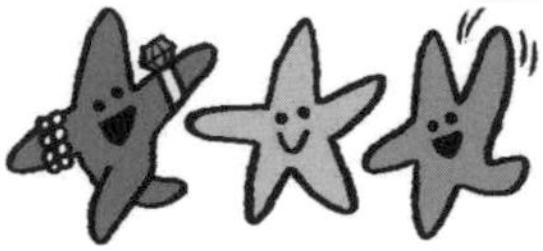

HarperAlley is an imprint of HarperCollins Publishers.

Crab and Snail: The Tidal Pool of Cool

 For information address HarperCollins Children's Books, a division of HarperCollins Publishers, 195 Broadway, New York, NY 10007.

www.harpercollinschildrens.com

ISBN 978-0-06-296216-4 (p-o-b)

ISBN 978-0-06-296217-1 (pbk.)

Typography by Chelsea C. Donaldson

22 23 24 25 26 RTLO 10 9 8 7 6 5 4 3 2 1

❖

First Edition

CRAB & SNAIL

The TIDAL POOL of COOL

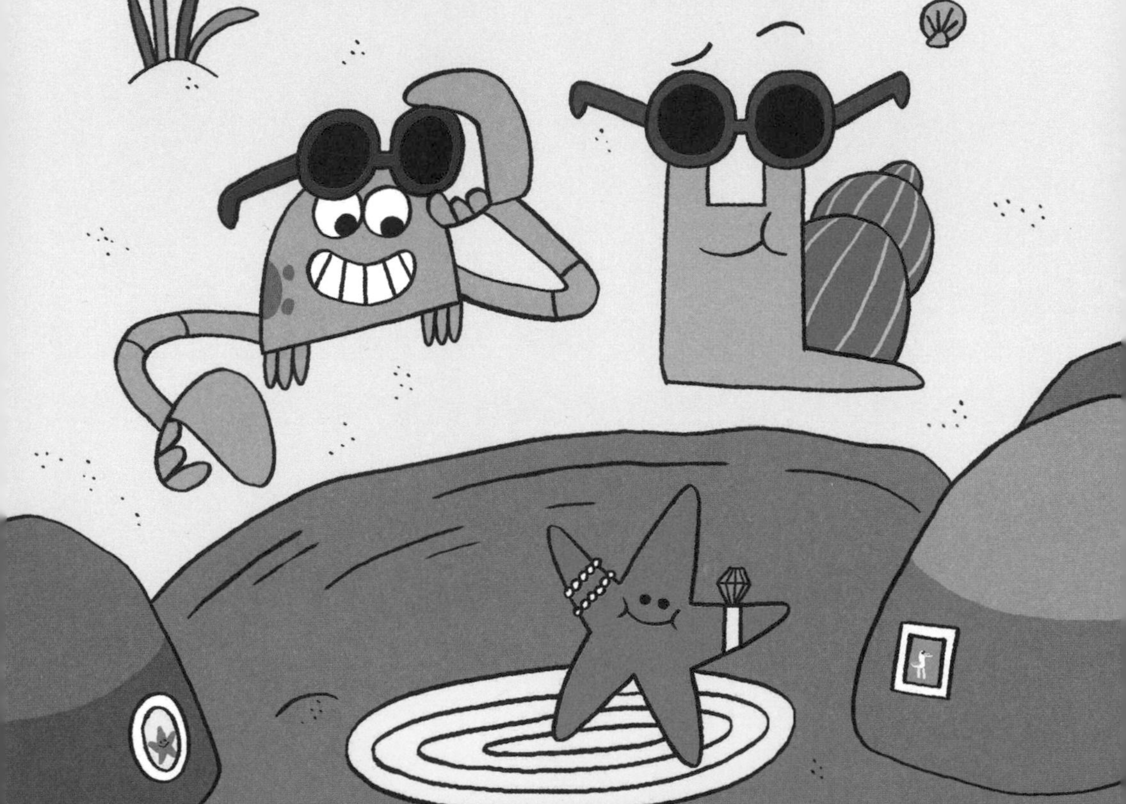

by Beth Ferry pictures by Jared Chapman

HARPER alley
An Imprint of HarperCollinsPublishers

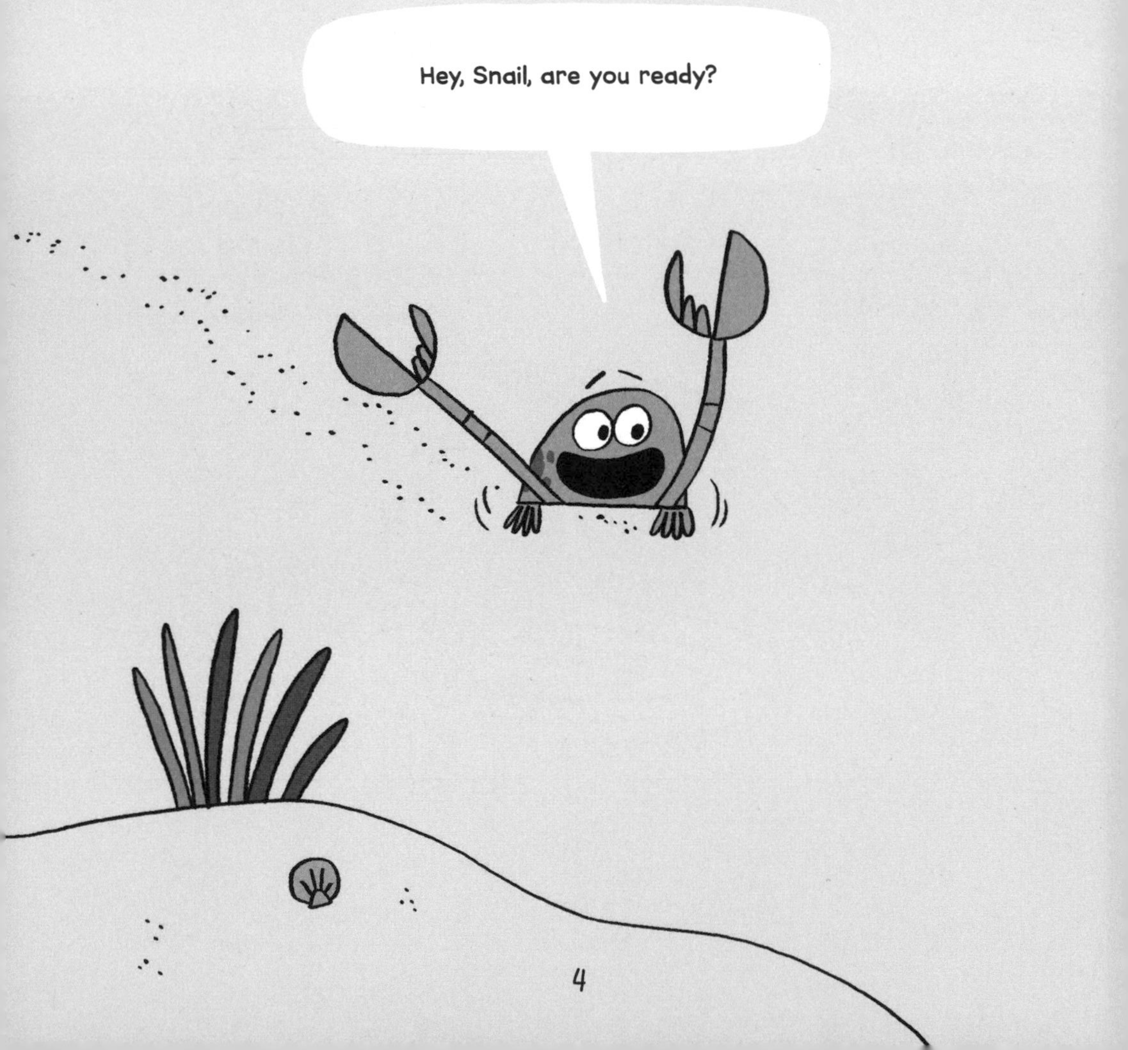
Hey, Snail, are you ready?

Ready for what?

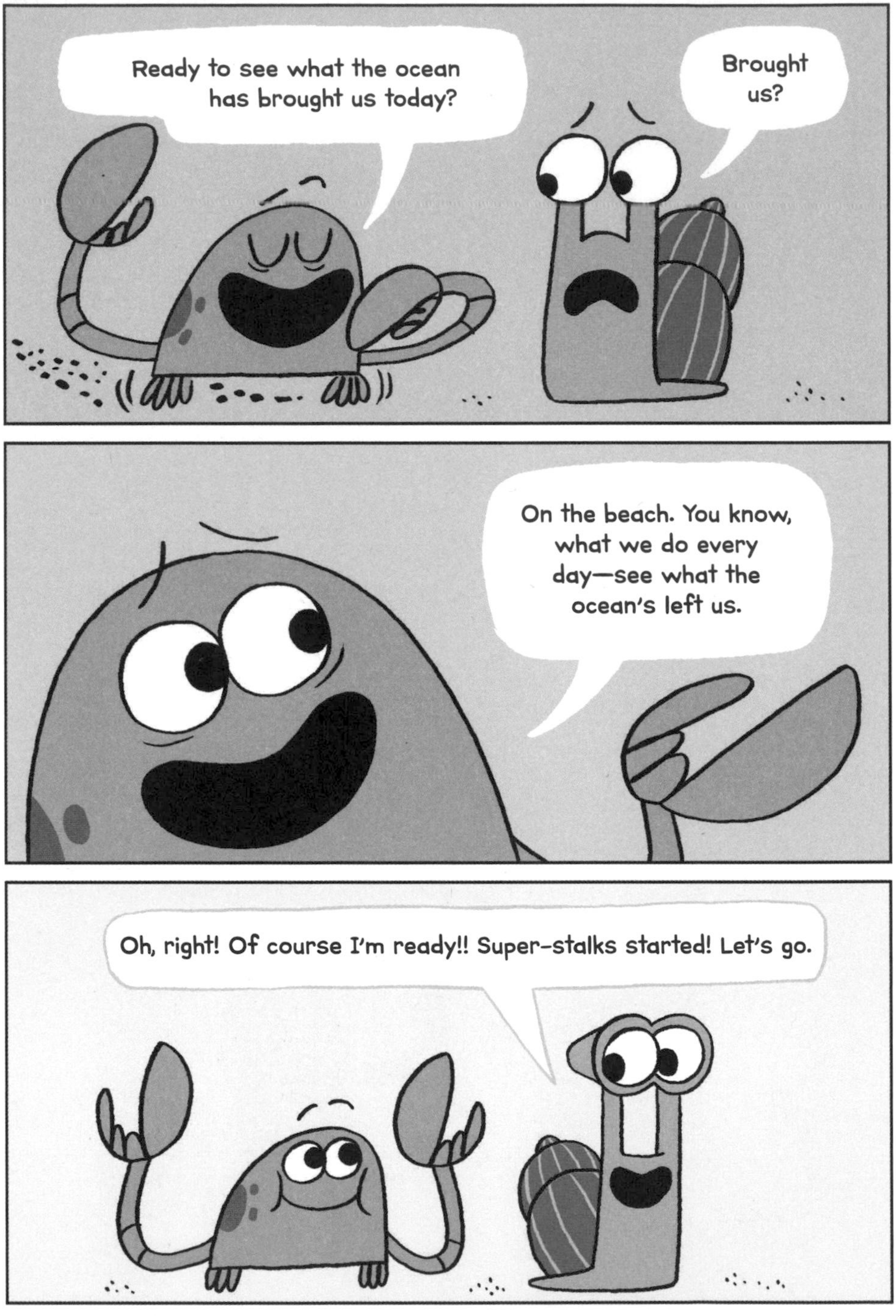
Ready to see what the ocean has brought us today?
Brought us?
On the beach. You know, what we do every day—see what the ocean's left us.
Oh, right! Of course I'm ready!! Super-stalks started! Let's go.

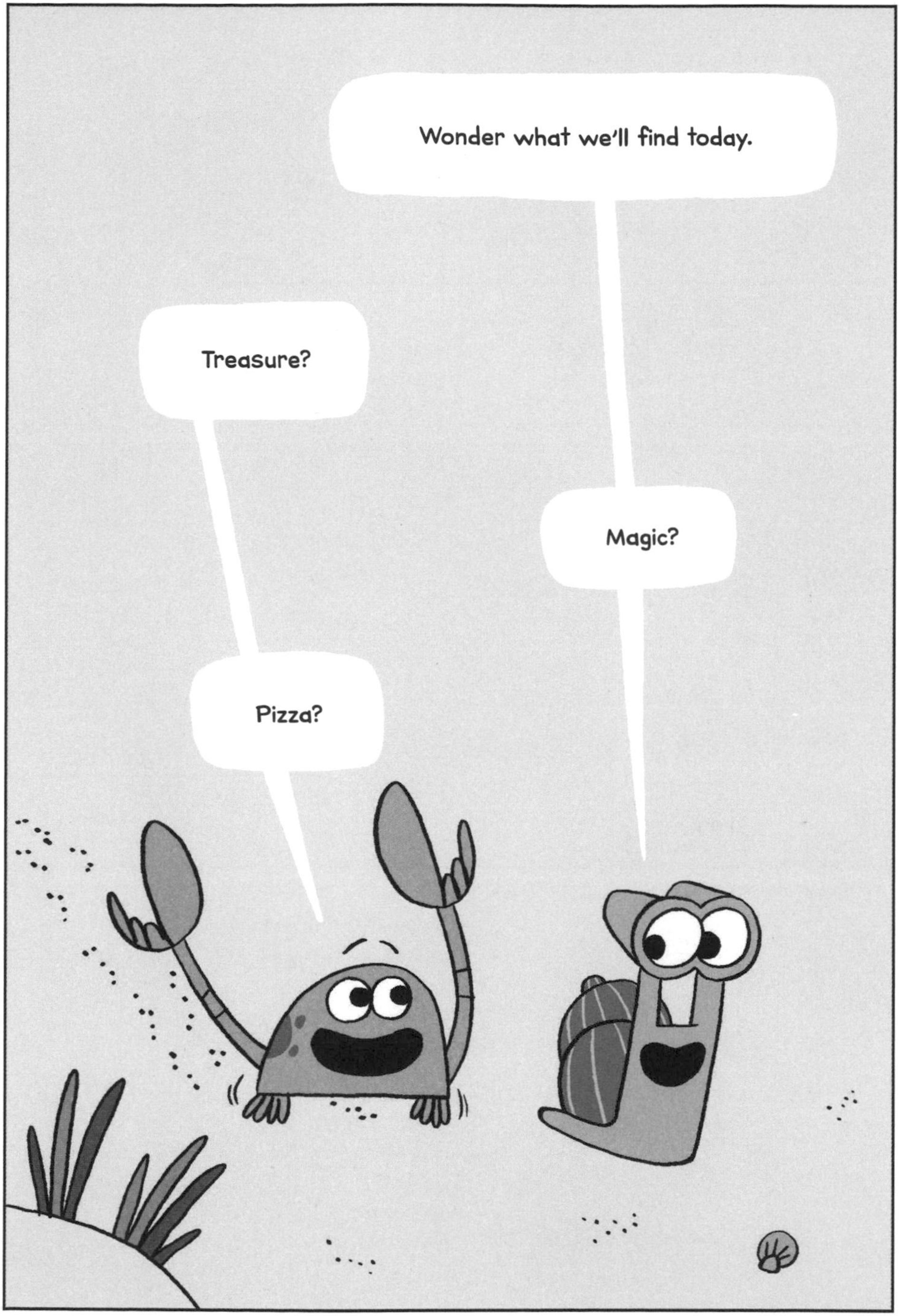
Wonder what we'll find today.
Treasure?
Magic?
Pizza?

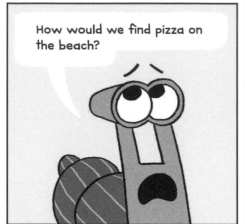

How would we find pizza on the beach?

I don't know. Maybe a pizza-loving bird dropped some.

No bird would ever drop something as yummy as a piece of pizza.

How do you know?

Did you already forget? I know everything.

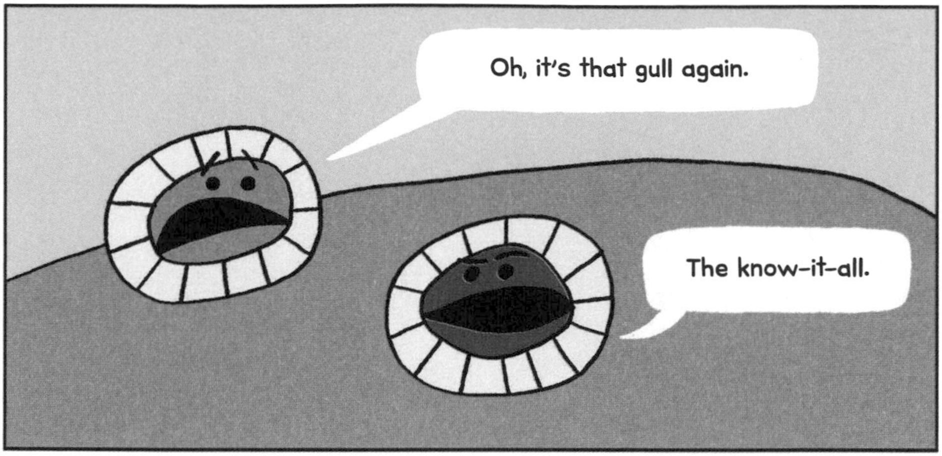
Oh, it's that gull again.
The know-it-all.

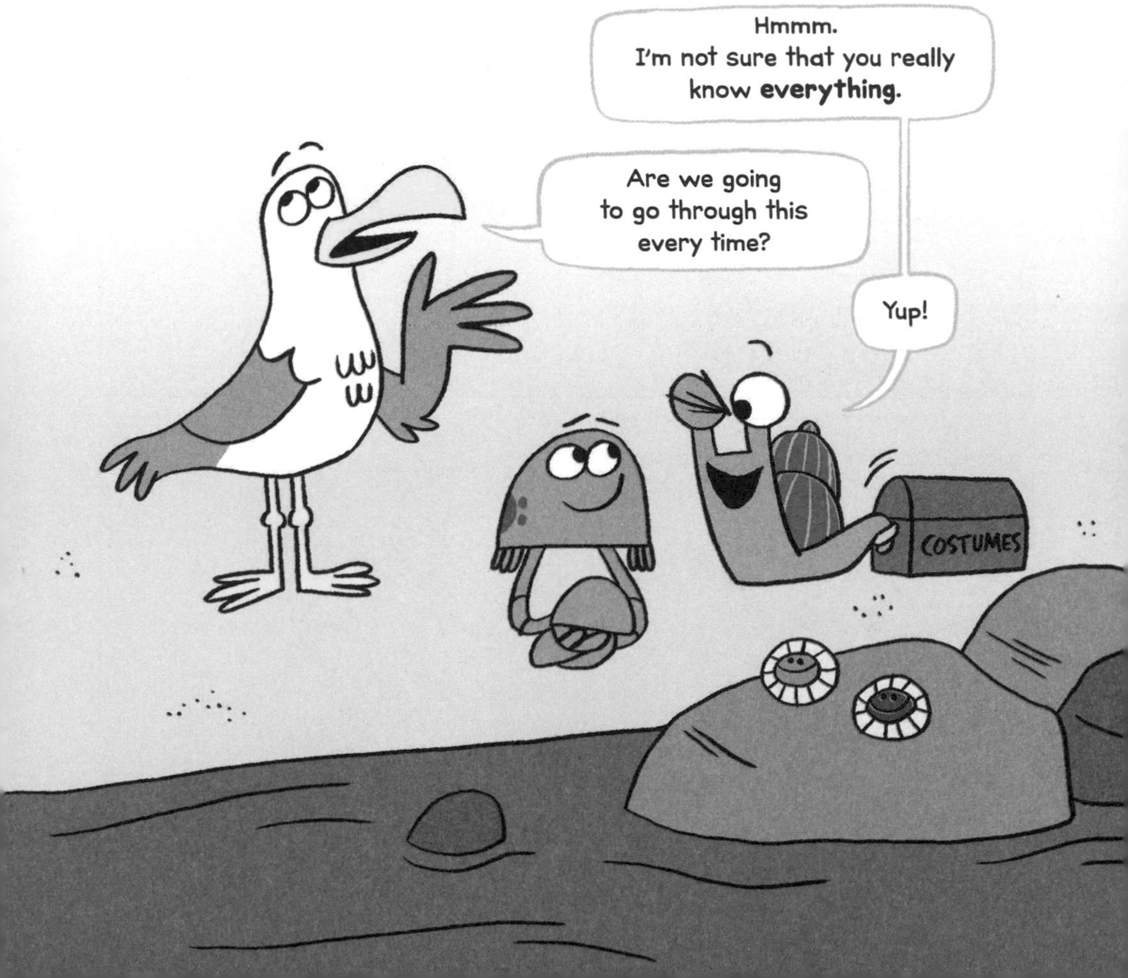
Hmmm.
I'm not sure that you really know **everything**.
Are we going to go through this every time?
Yup!
COSTUMES

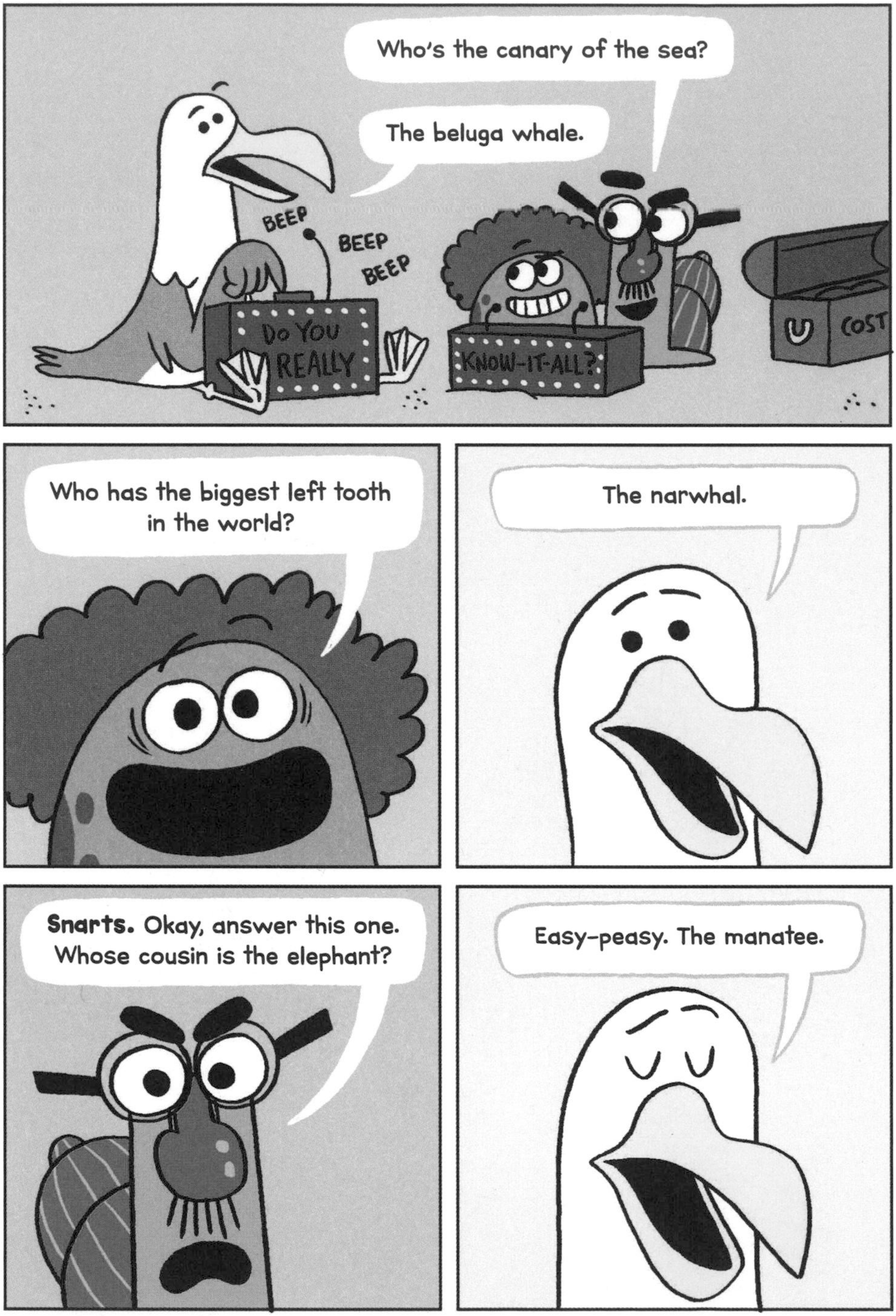
Who's the canary of the sea?
The beluga whale.
BEEP
BEEP
BEEP
DO YOU REALLY
KNOW-IT-ALL?
U
COST
Who has the biggest left tooth in the world?
The narwhal.
Snarts. Okay, answer this one. Whose cousin is the elephant?
Easy-peasy. The manatee.

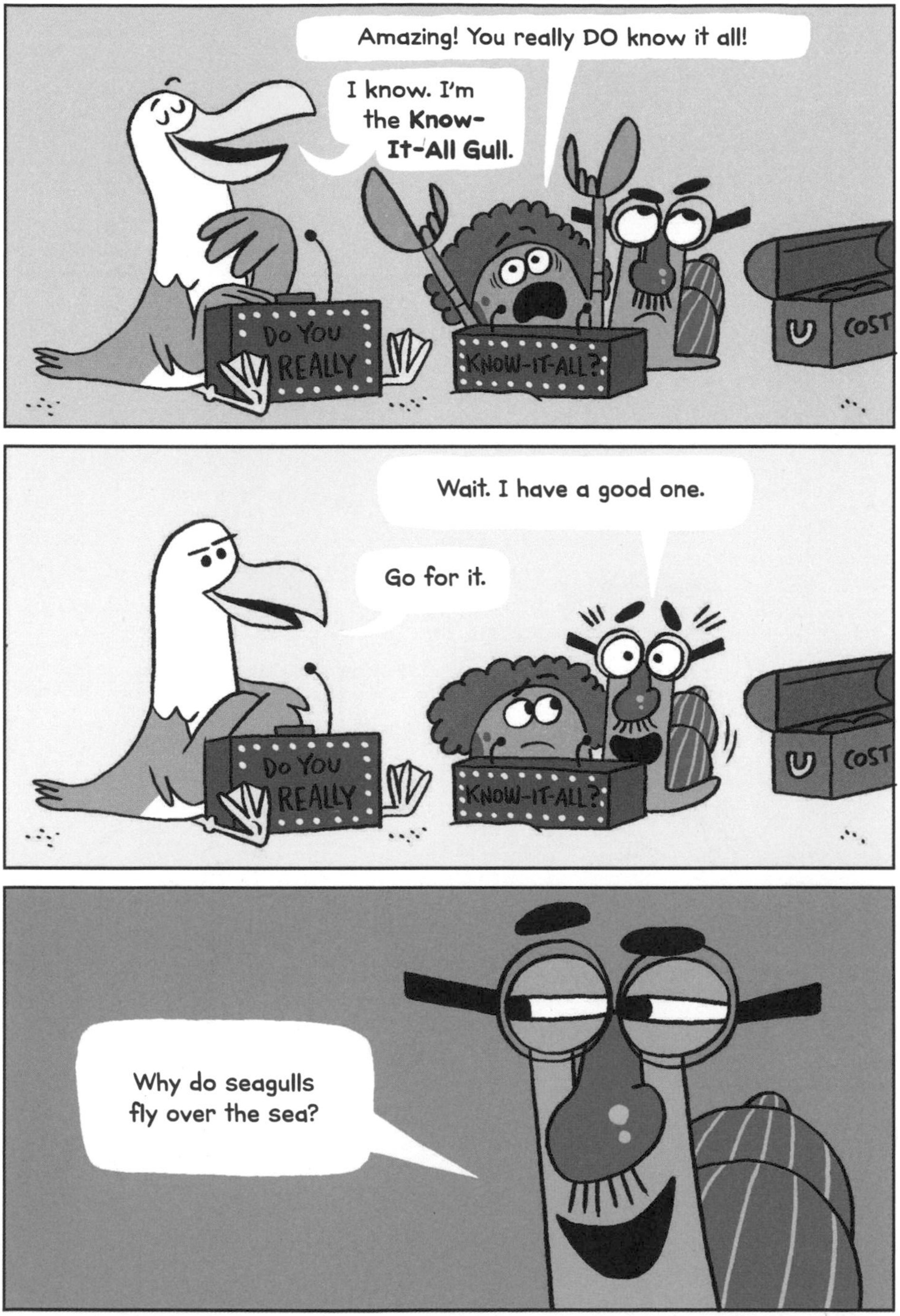
Amazing! You really DO know it all!
I know. I'm the **Know-It-All Gull.**
DO YOU REALLY
KNOW-IT-ALL?
U COST
Wait. I have a good one.
Go for it.
DO YOU REALLY
KNOW-IT-ALL?
U COST
Why do seagulls fly over the sea?

Um.
Er.
Grrr.
Arrr!
Sigh. I don't know.
If they flew over the bay, they'd be bagels! Get it? Bay-gulls?? **Tee hee!!**
DO YOU REALLY
KNOW-IT-ALL?
COSTUMES

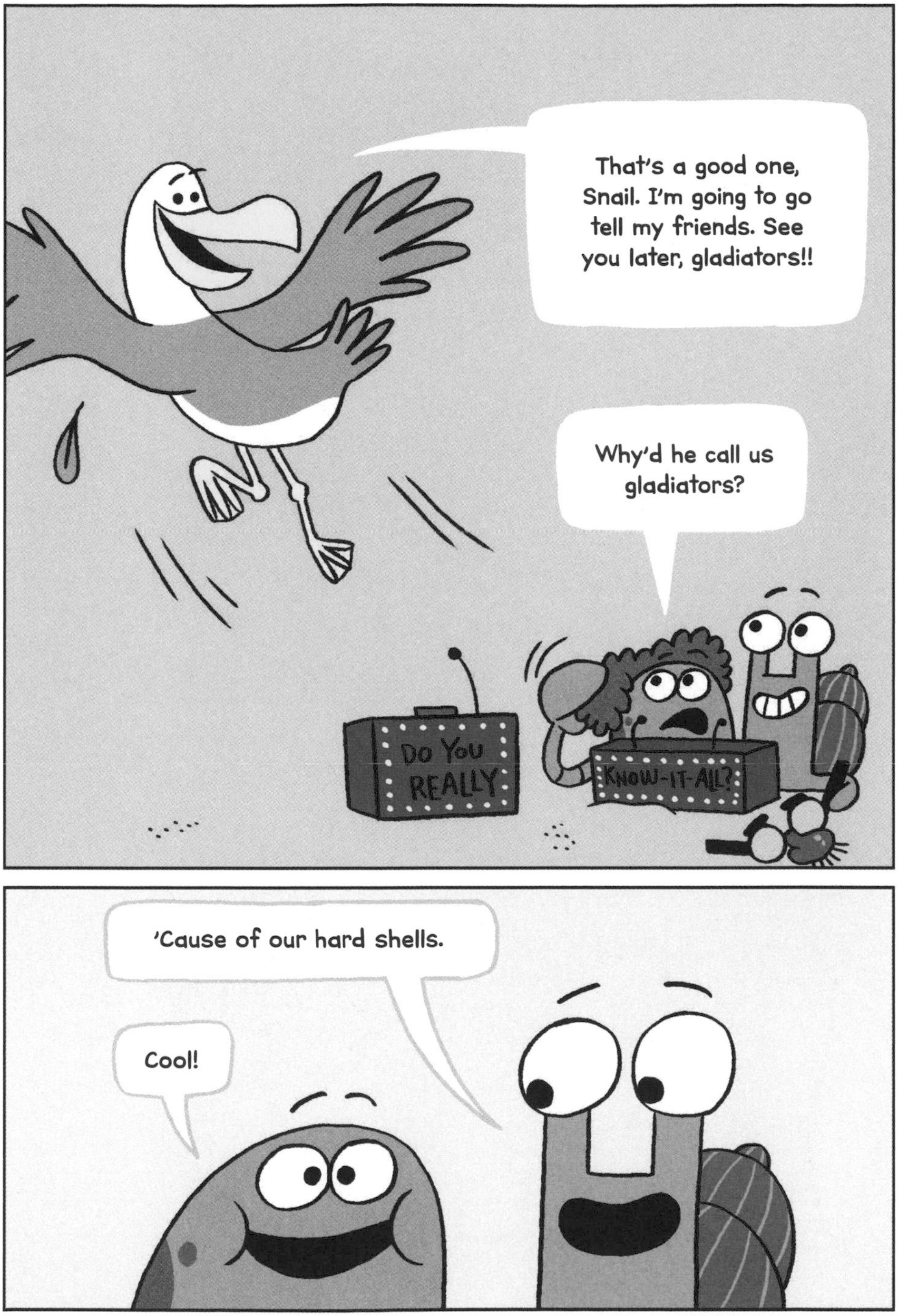
That's a good one, Snail. I'm going to go tell my friends. See you later, gladiators!!
Why'd he call us gladiators?
DO YOU REALLY
KNOW-IT-ALL?
'Cause of our hard shells.
Cool!

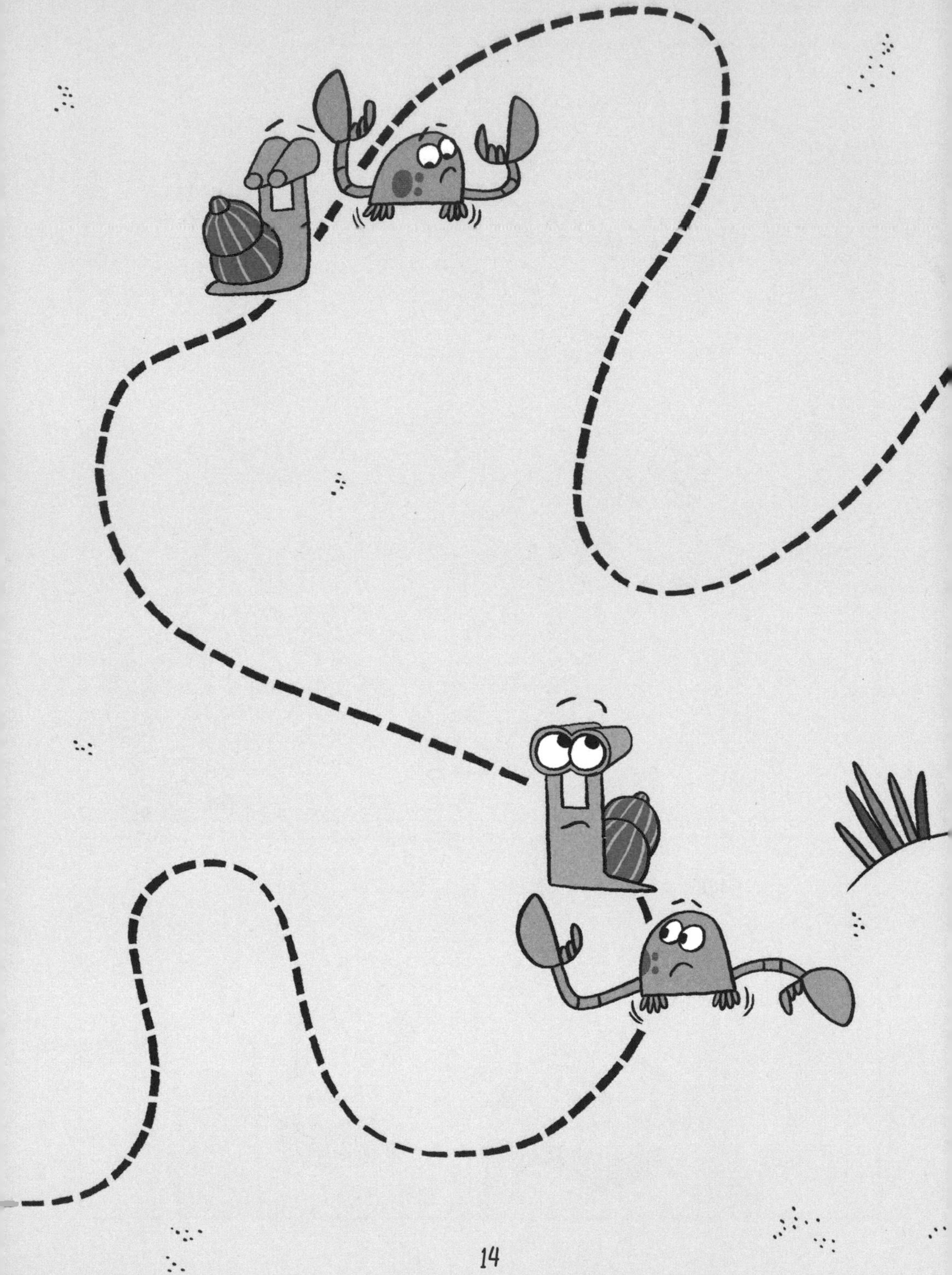

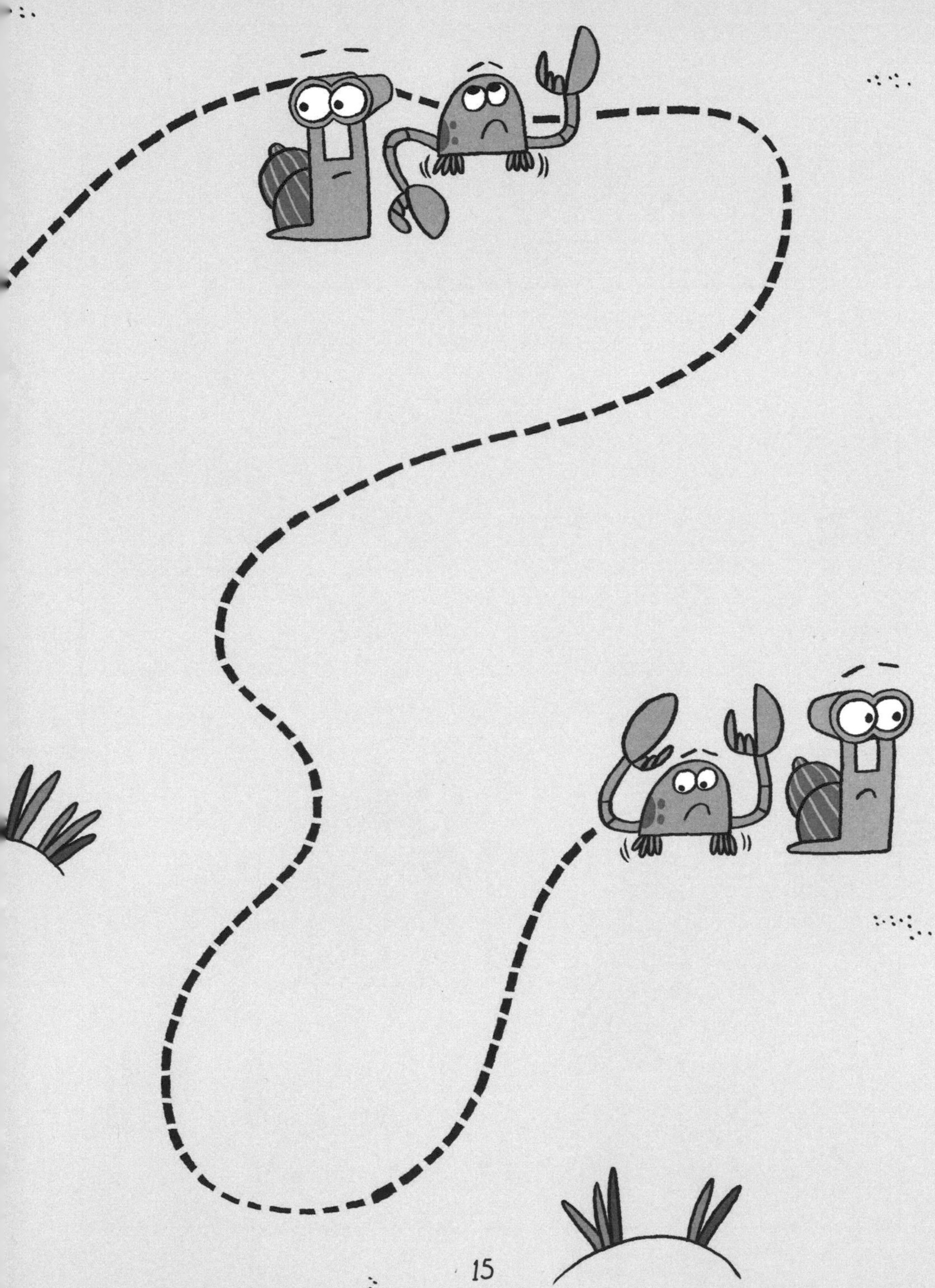

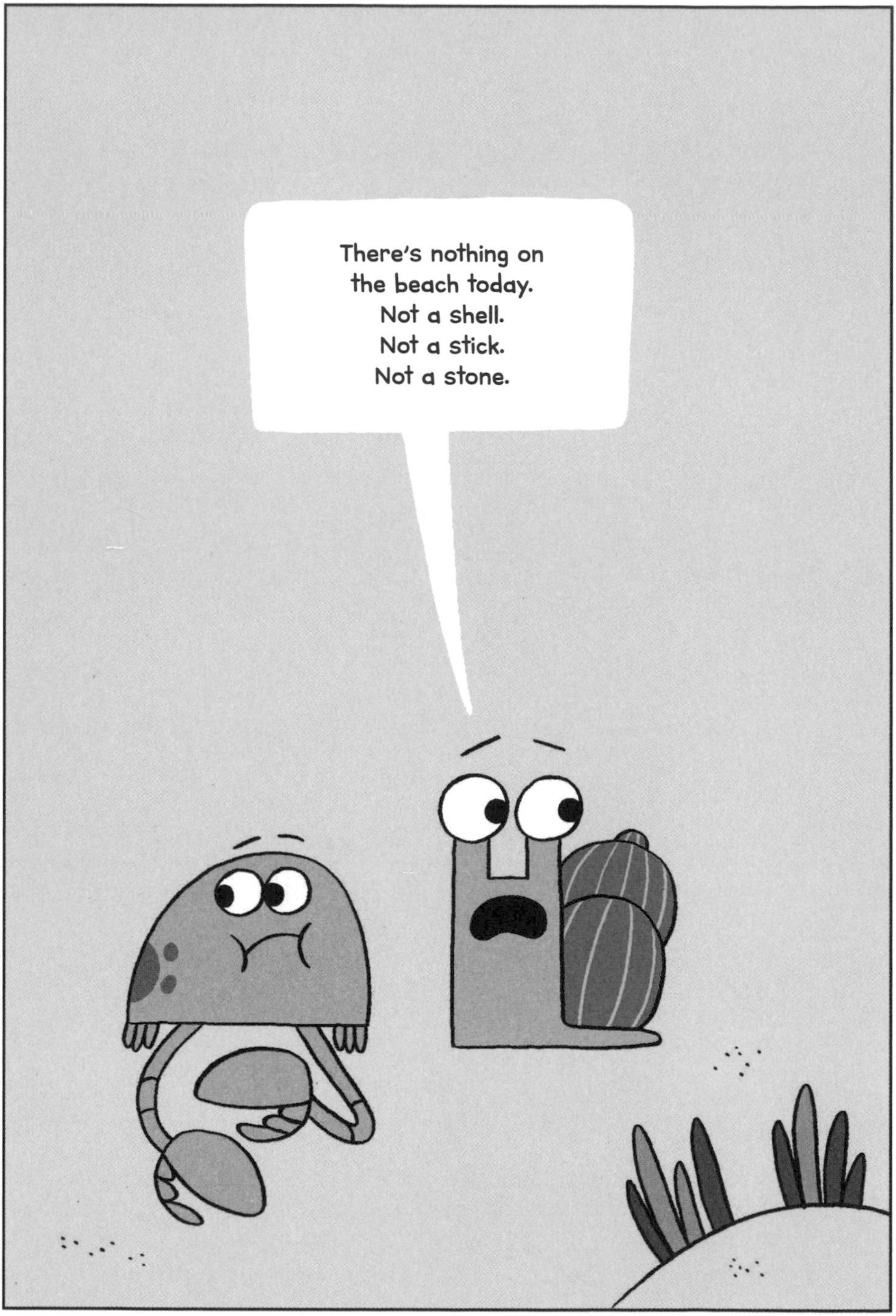
There's nothing on the beach today. Not a shell. Not a stick. Not a stone.

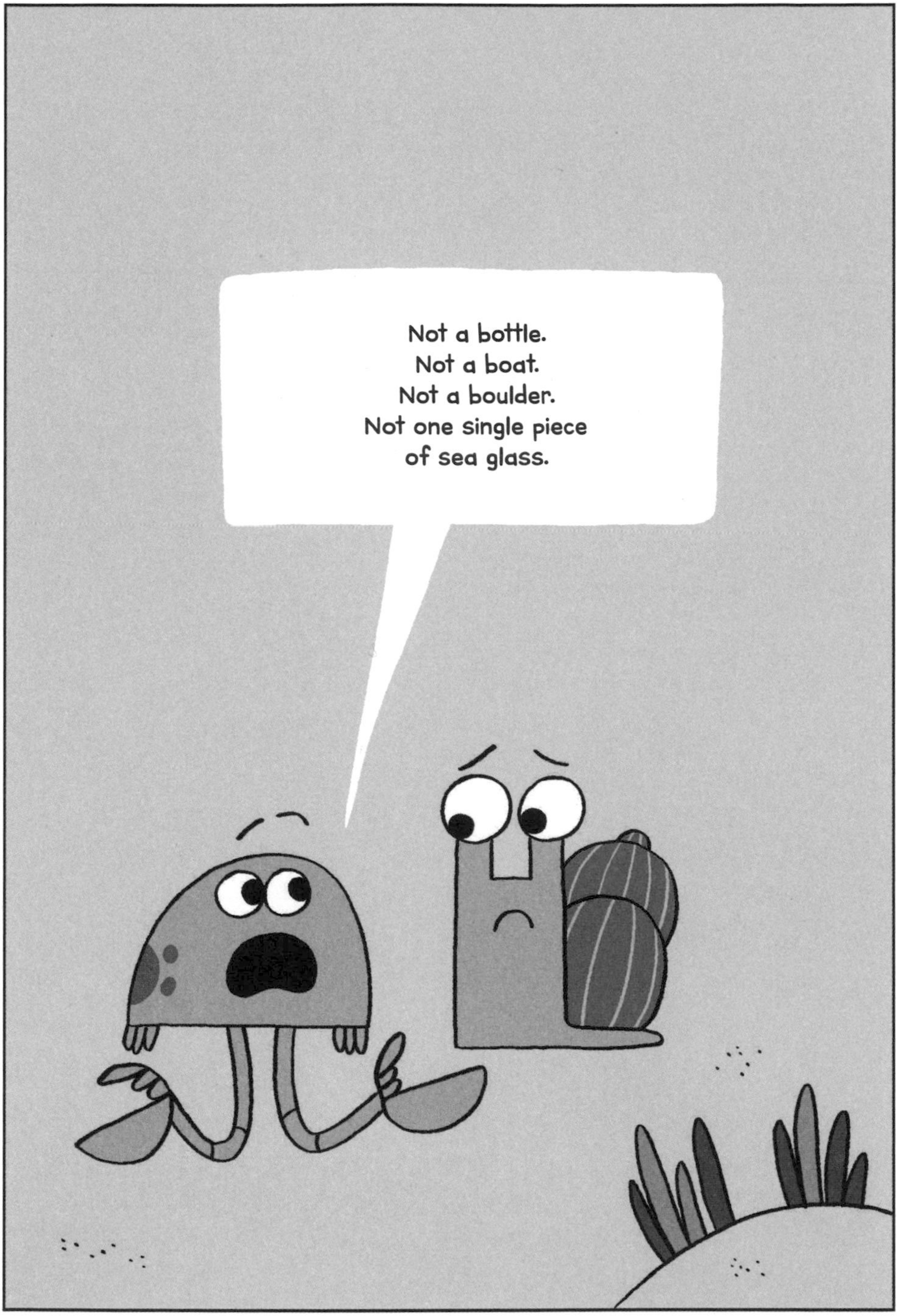
Not a bottle.
Not a boat.
Not a boulder.
Not one single piece
of sea glass.

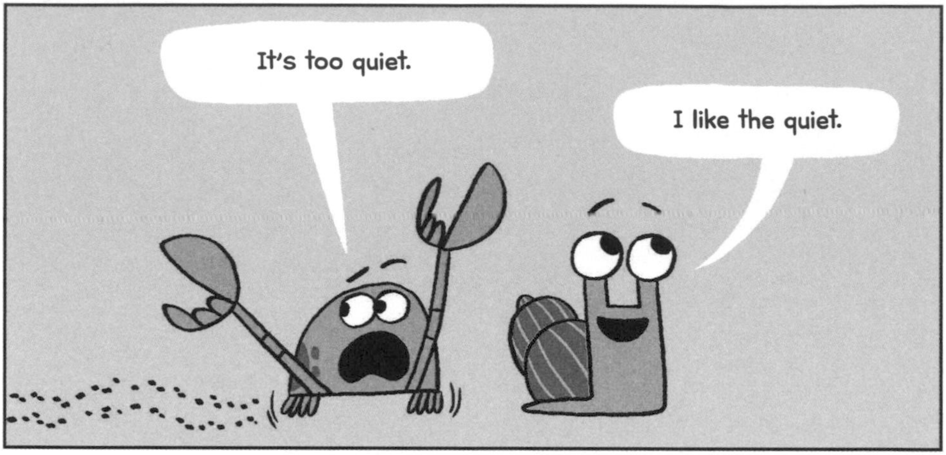
It's too quiet.
I like the quiet.

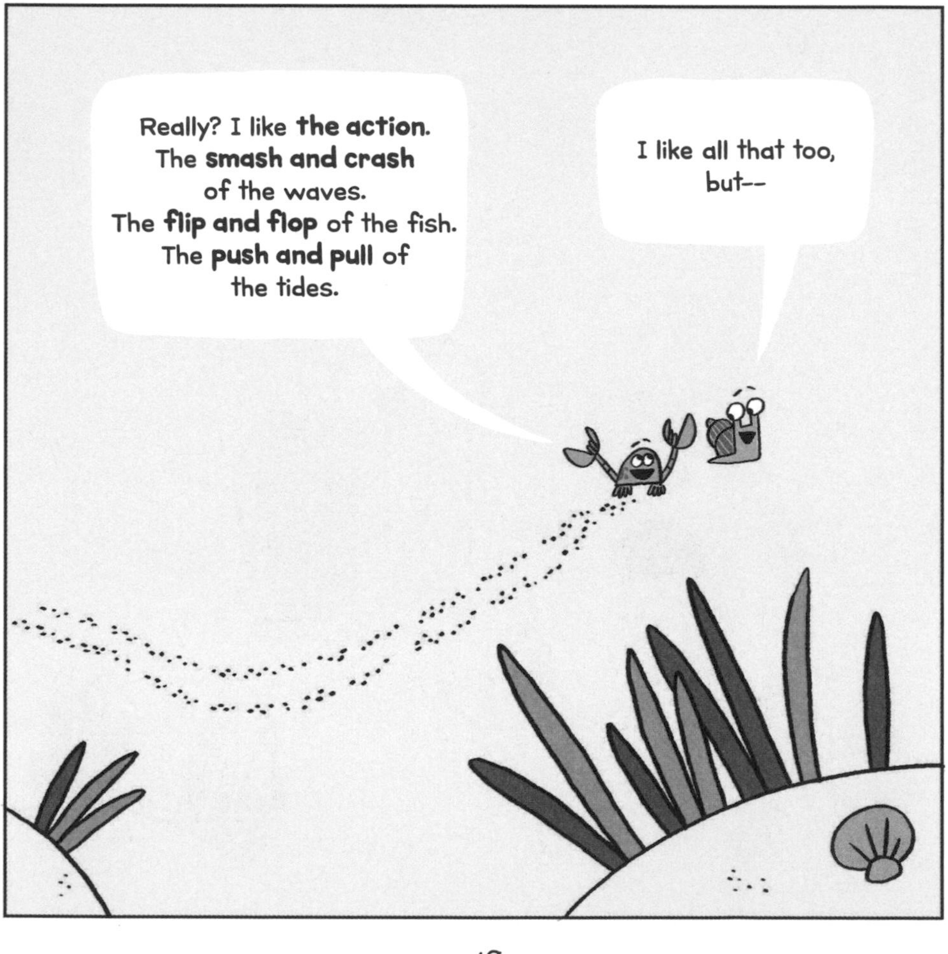
Really? I like **the action.** The **smash and crash** of the waves. The **flip and flop** of the fish. The **push and pull** of the tides.
I like all that too, but--

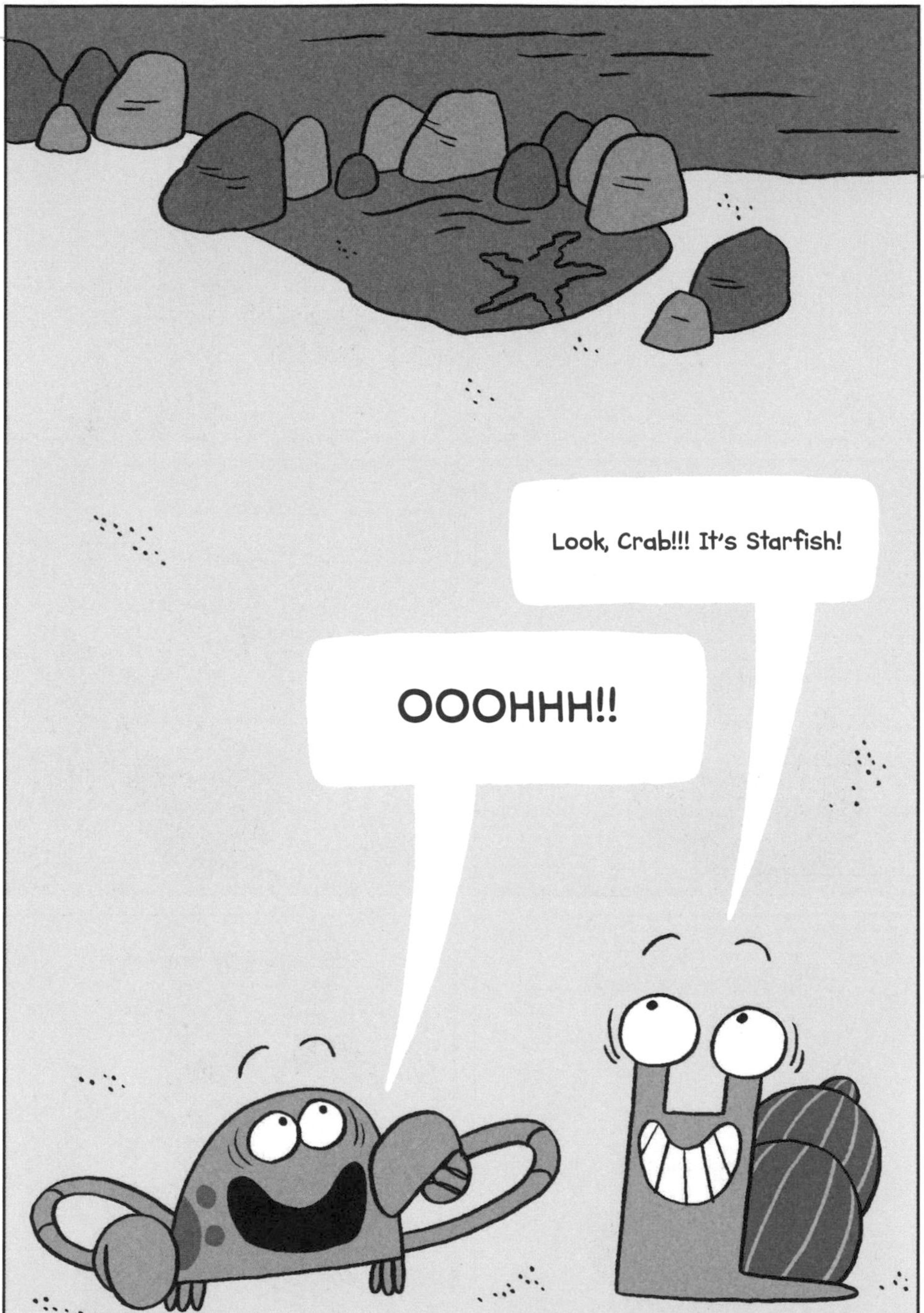
Look, Crab!!! It's Starfish!
OOOHHH!!

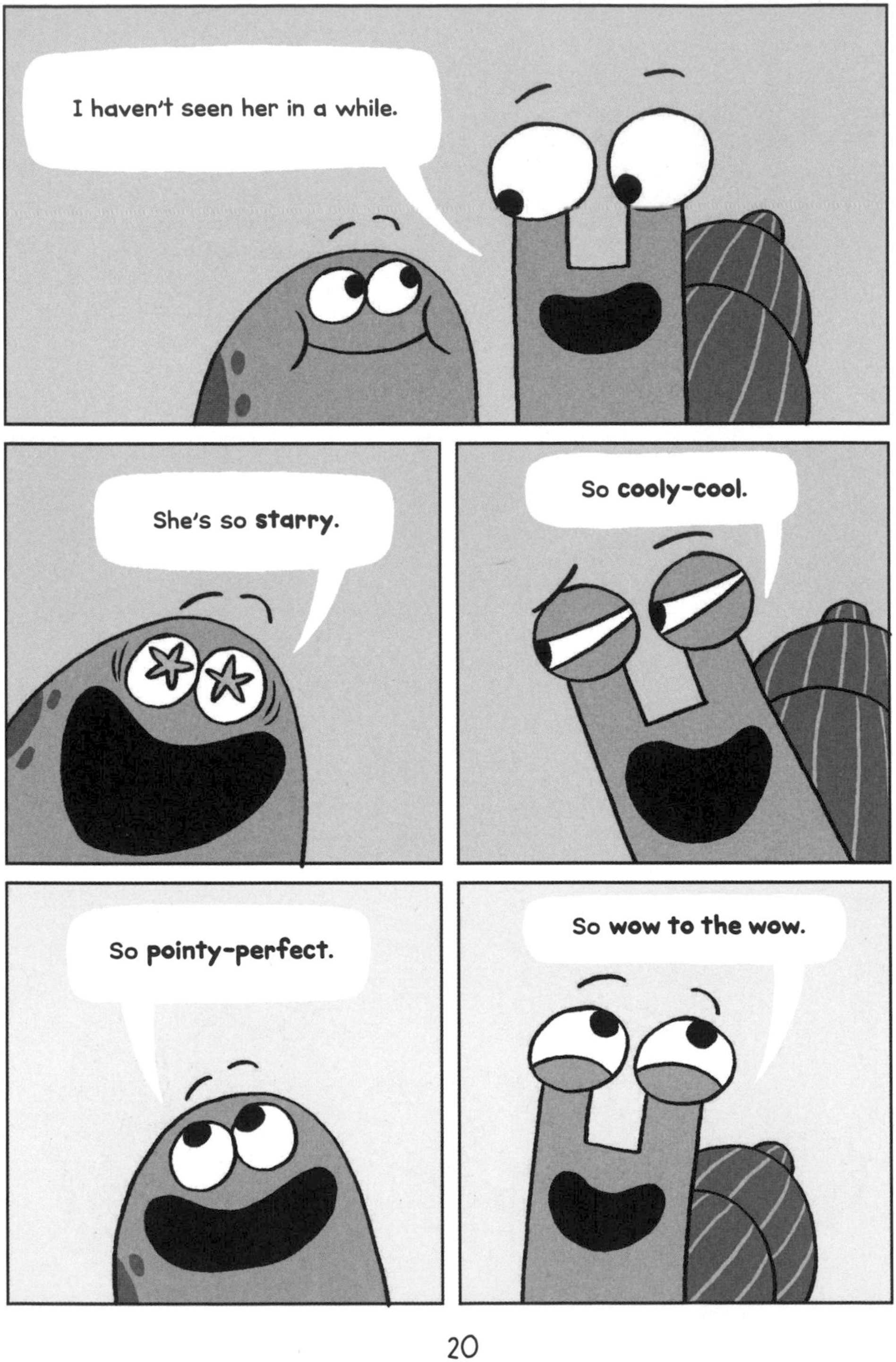
I haven't seen her in a while.
She's so **starry**.
So **cooly-cool**.
So **pointy-perfect**.
So **wow to the wow**.

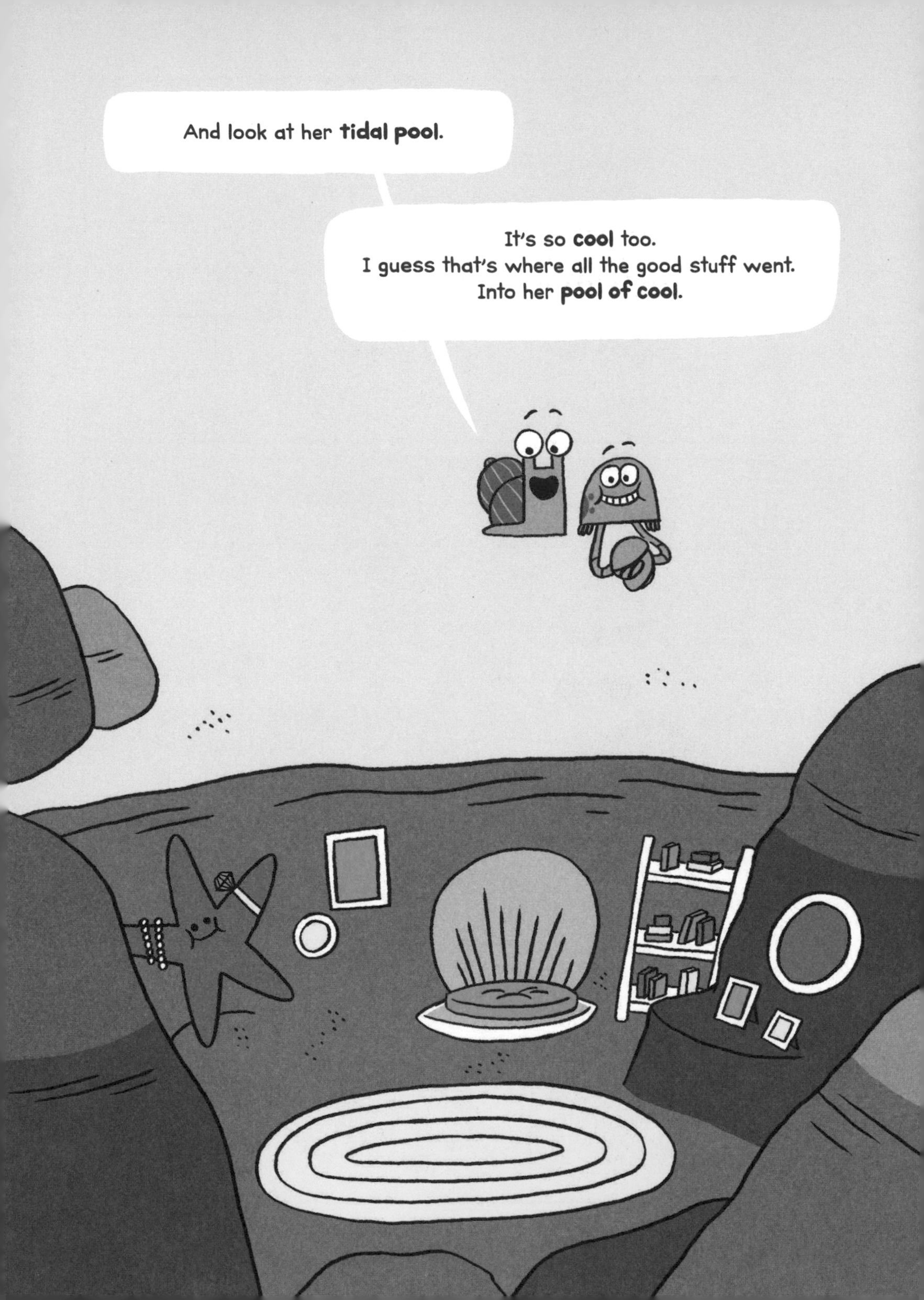
And look at her **tidal pool**.
It's so **cool** too. I guess that's where all the good stuff went. Into her **pool of cool**.

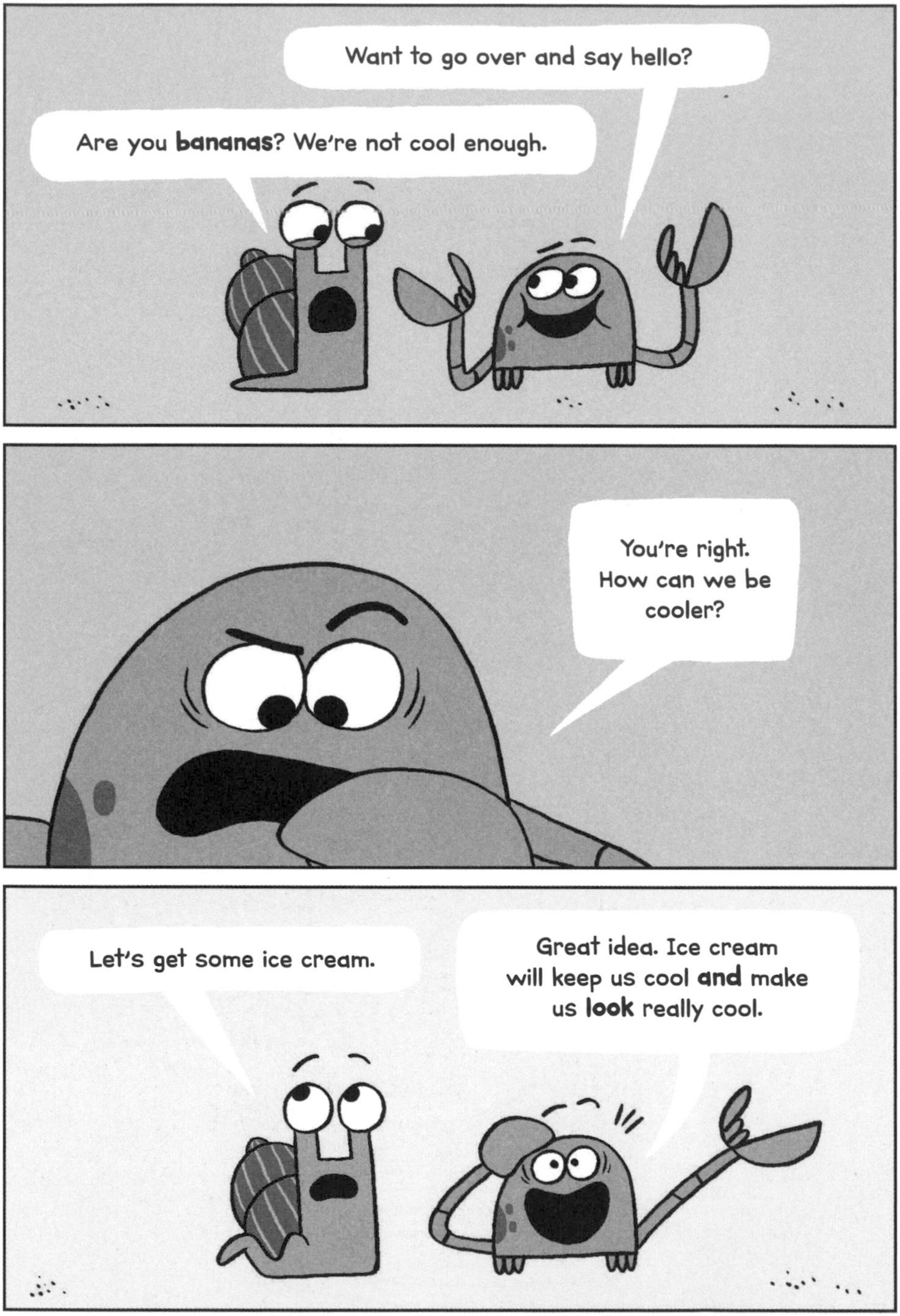
Want to go over and say hello?
Are you **bananas**? We're not cool enough.
You're right. How can we be cooler?
Let's get some ice cream.
Great idea. Ice cream will keep us cool **and** make us **look** really cool.

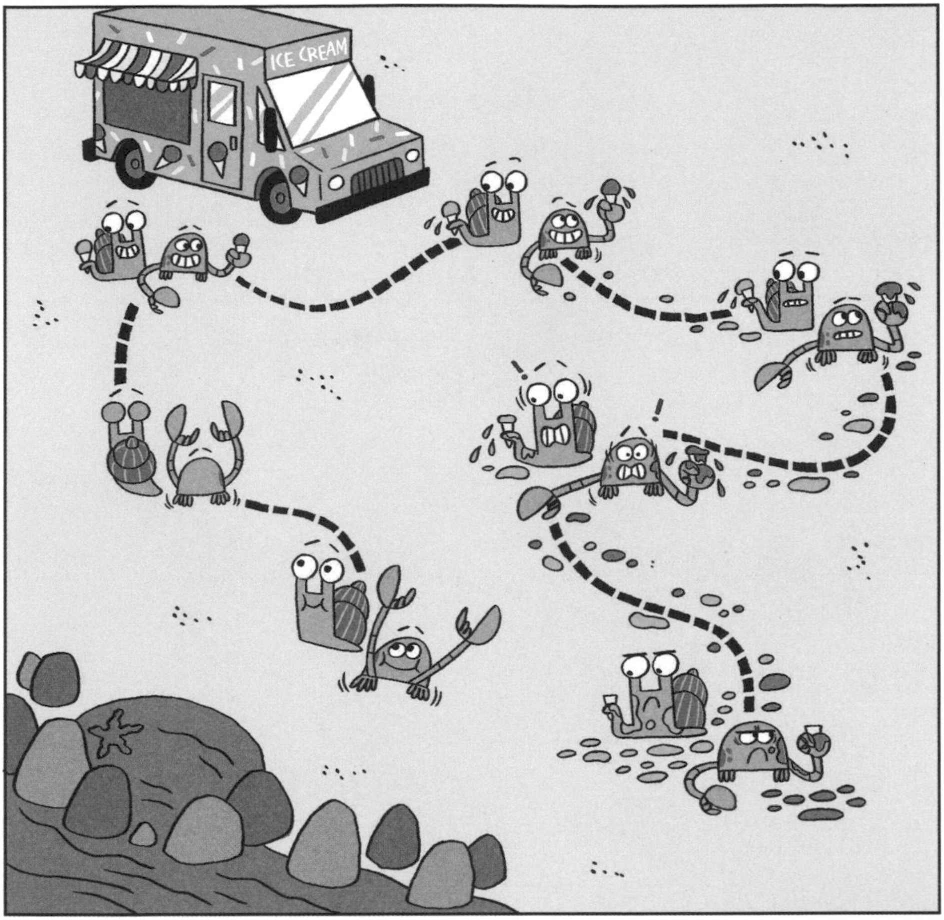
ICE CREAM

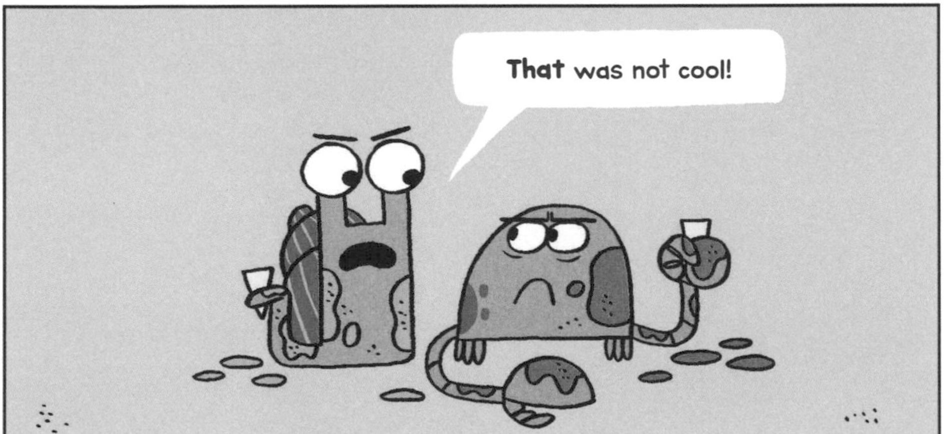
That was not cool!

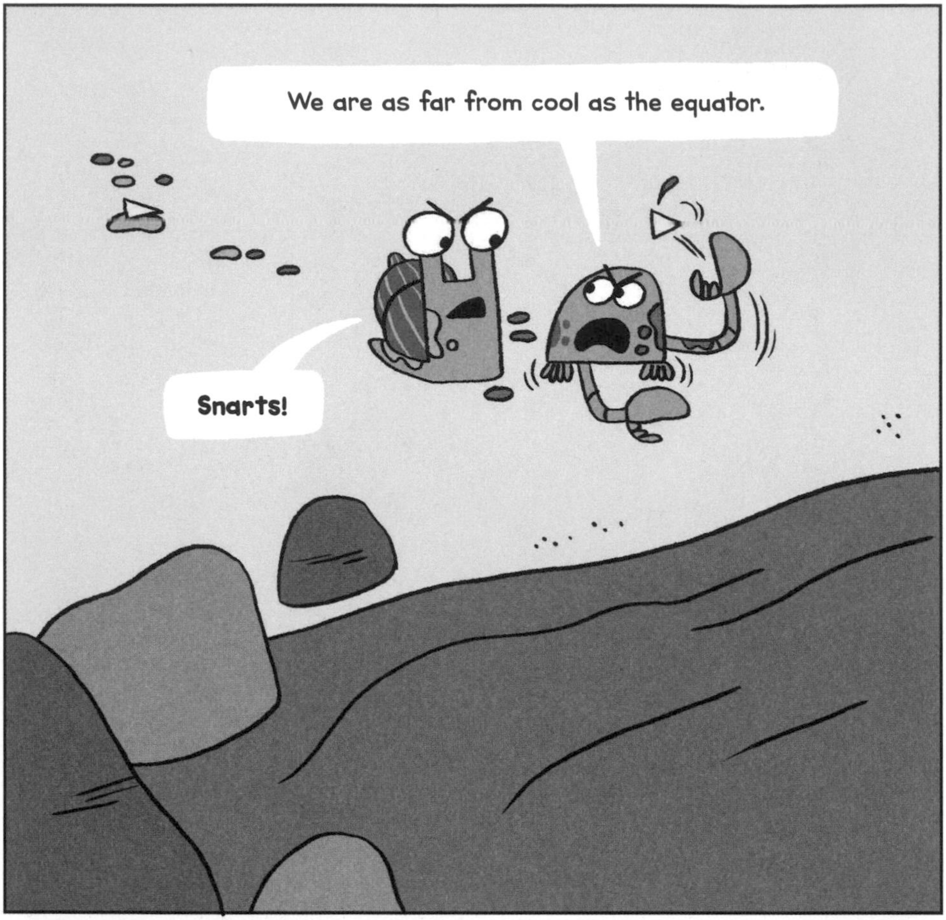
We are as far from cool as the equator.
Snarts!

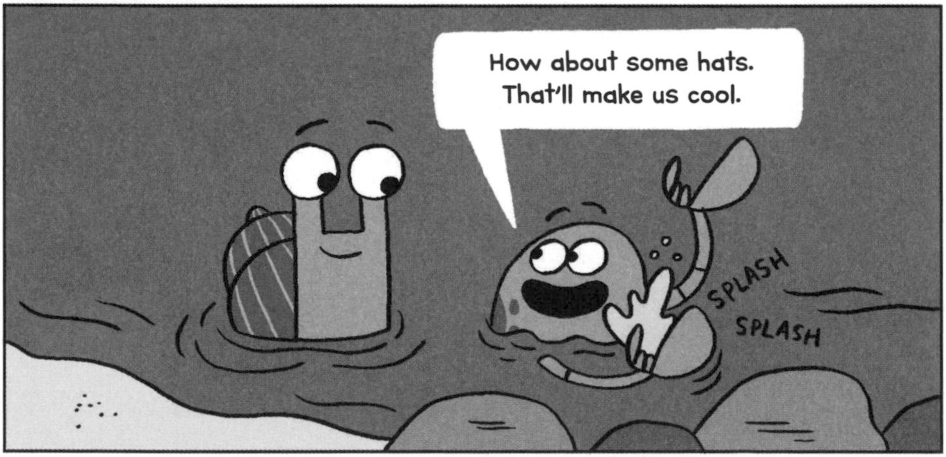
How about some hats.
That'll make us cool.
SPLASH
SPLASH

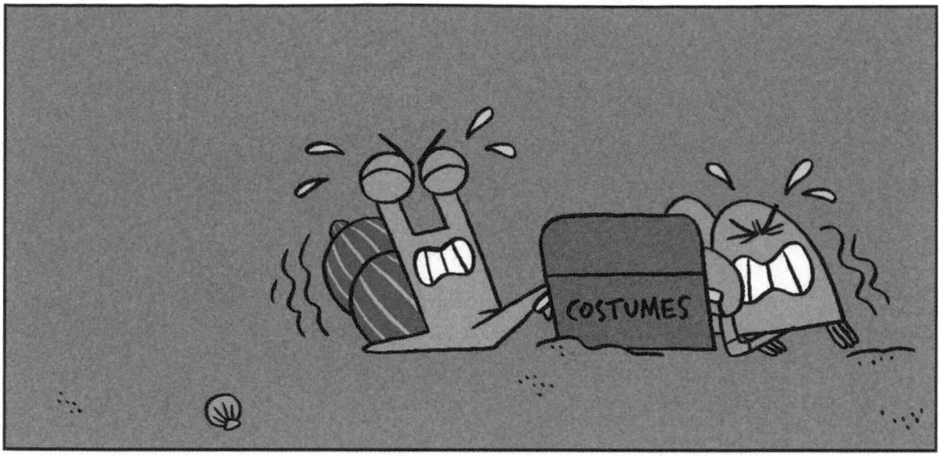
COSTUMES

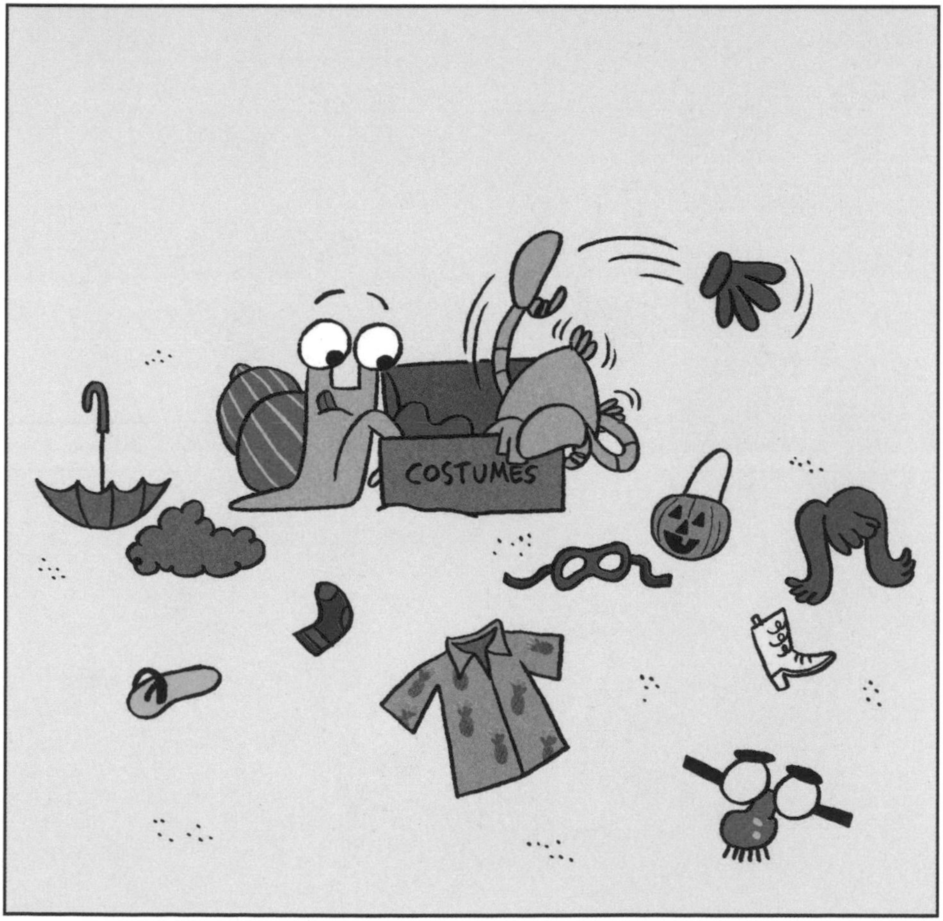
COSTUMES

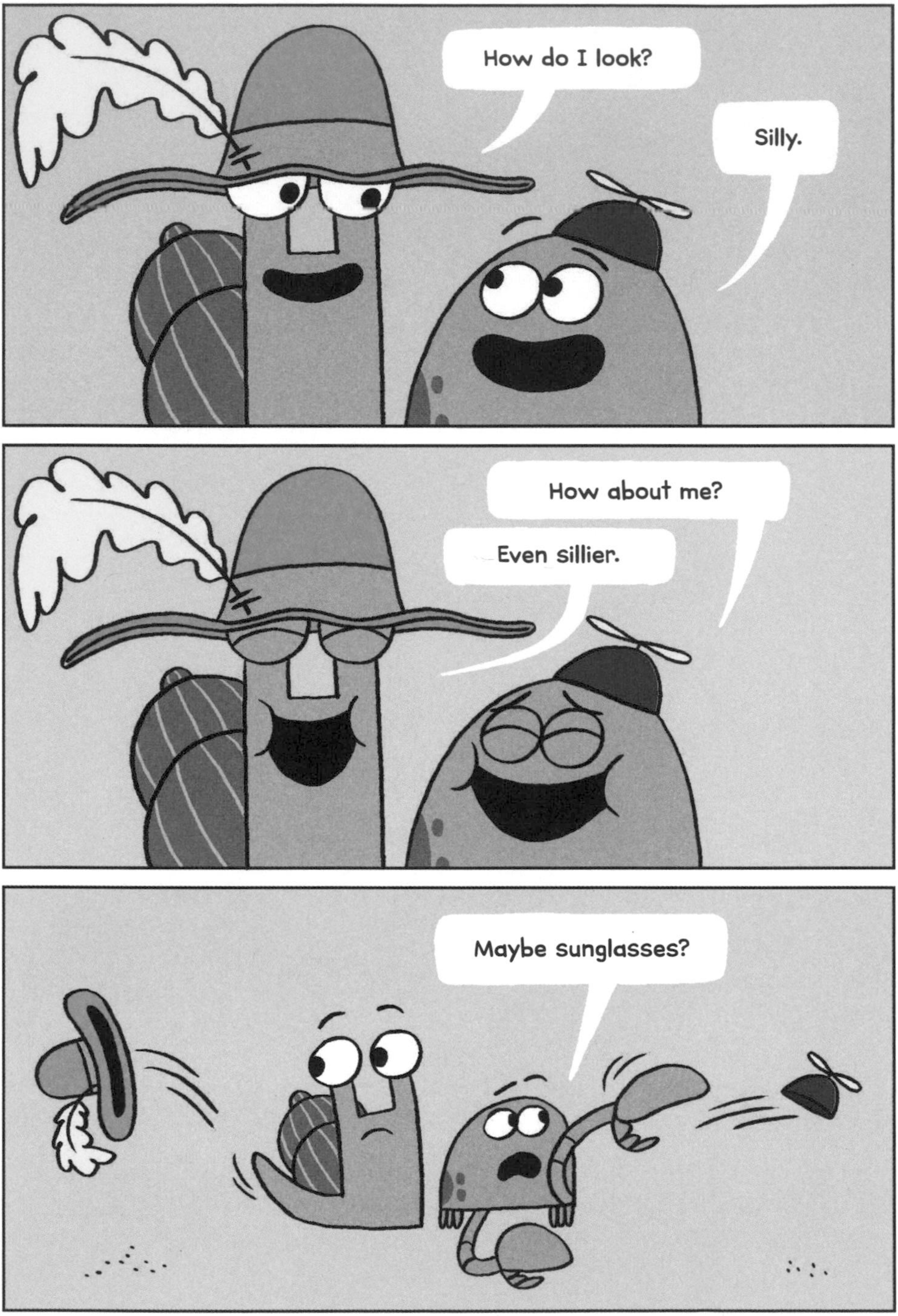
How do I look?
Silly.
How about me?
Even sillier.
Maybe sunglasses?

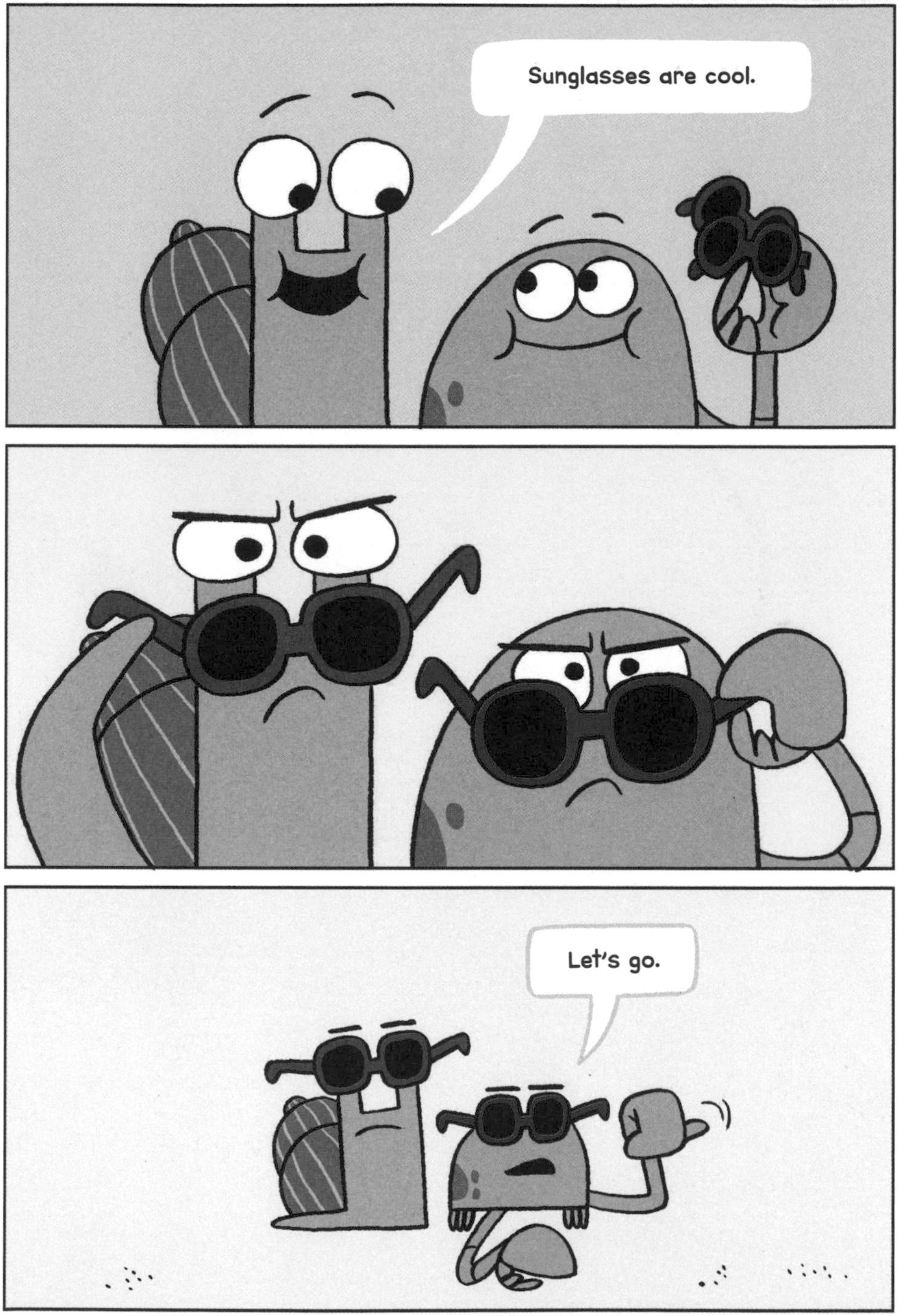
Sunglasses are cool.
Let's go.

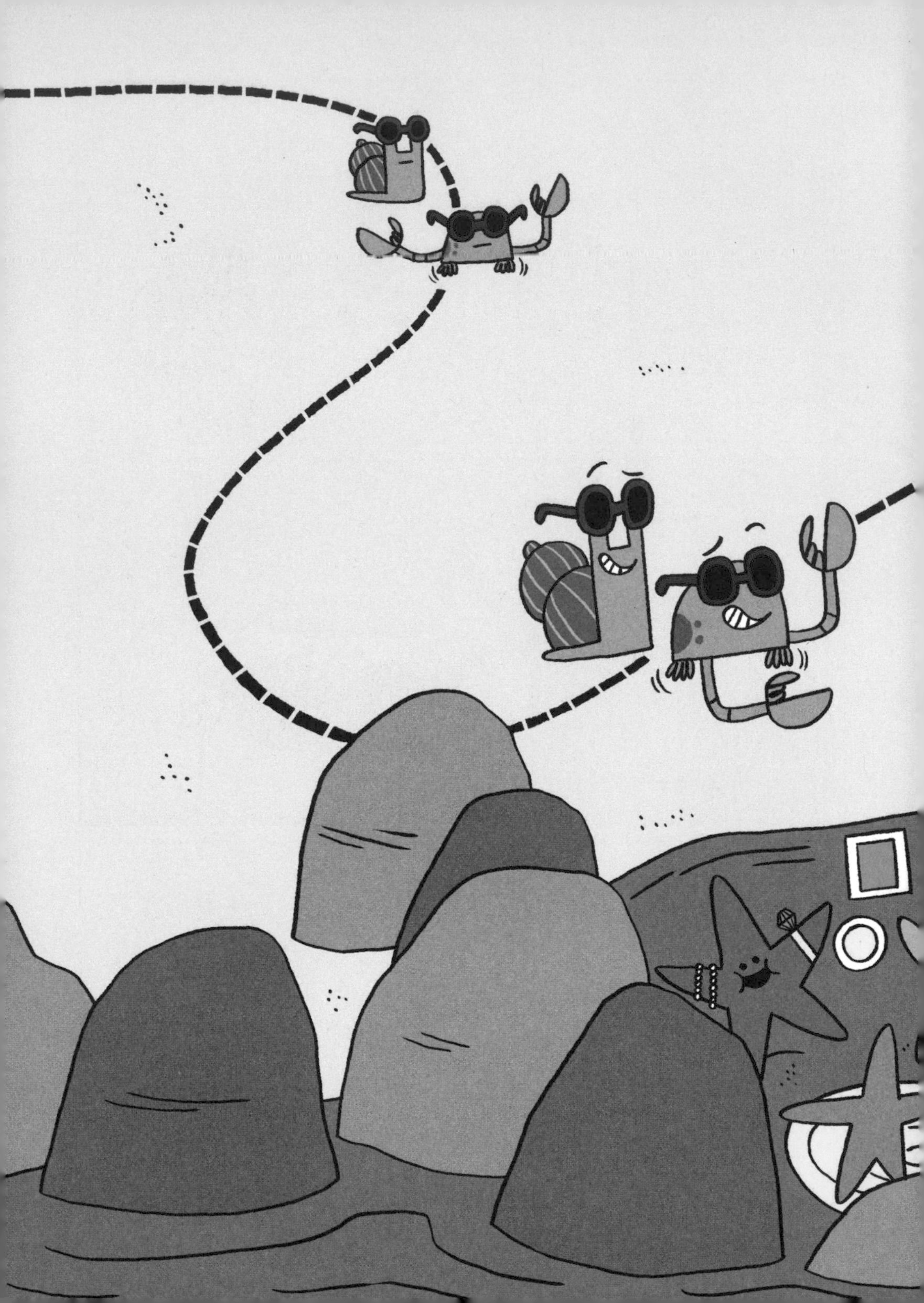

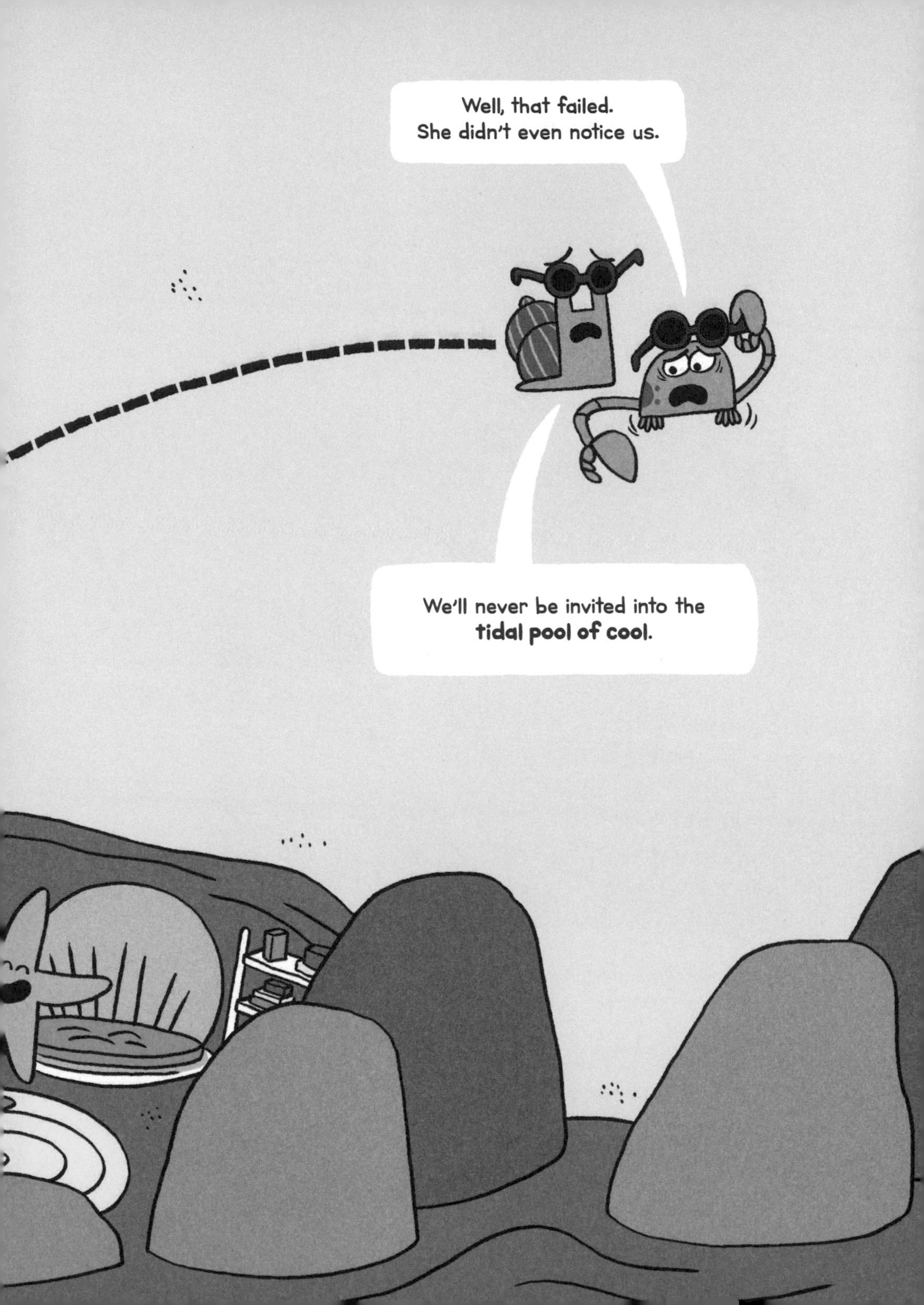
Well, that failed. She didn't even notice us.
We'll never be invited into the **tidal pool of cool**.

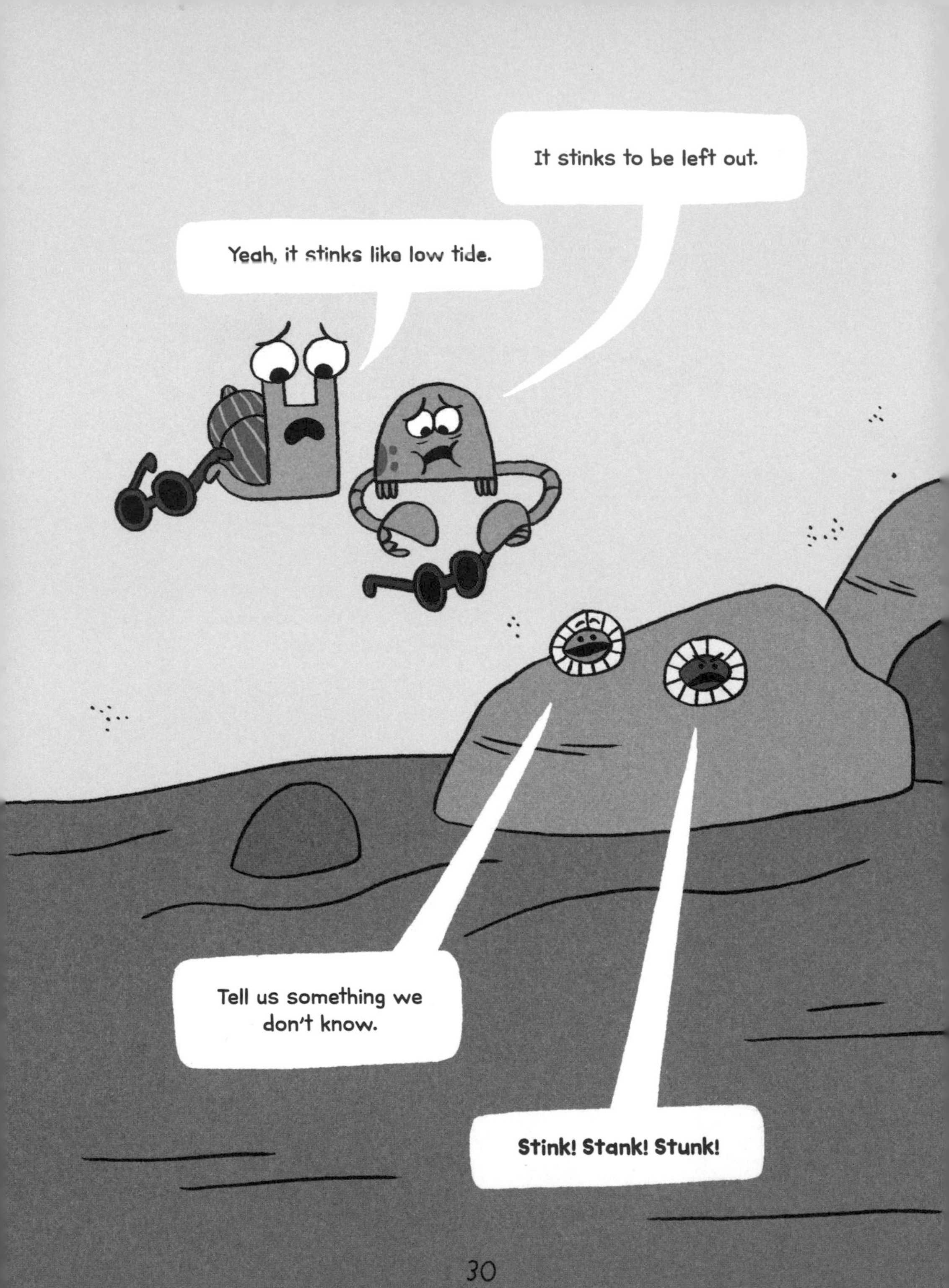
It stinks to be left out.
Yeah, it stinks like low tide.
Tell us something we don't know.
Stink! Stank! Stunk!

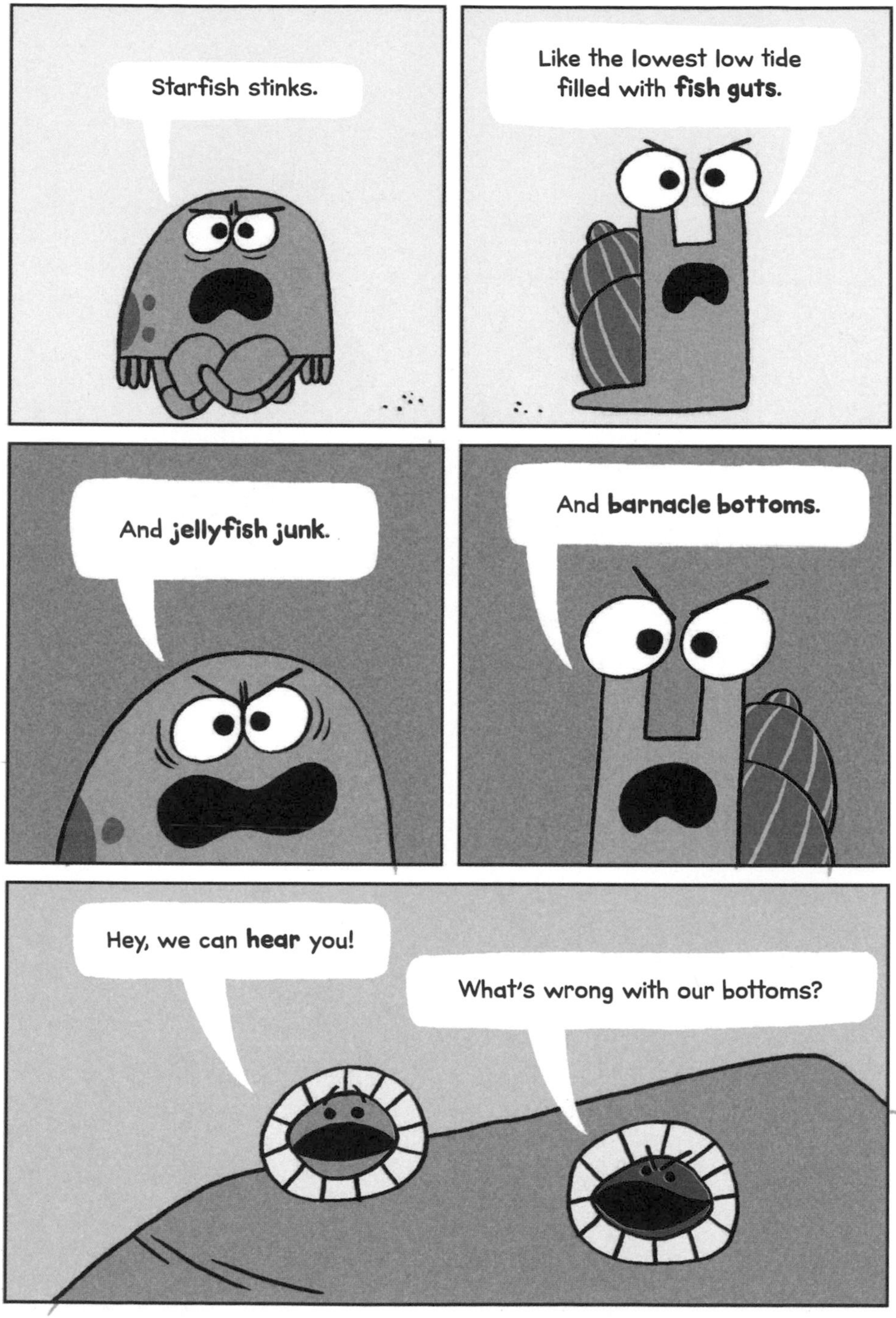
Starfish stinks.
Like the lowest low tide filled with **fish guts.**
And **jellyfish junk.**
And **barnacle bottoms.**
Hey, we can **hear** you!
What's wrong with our bottoms?

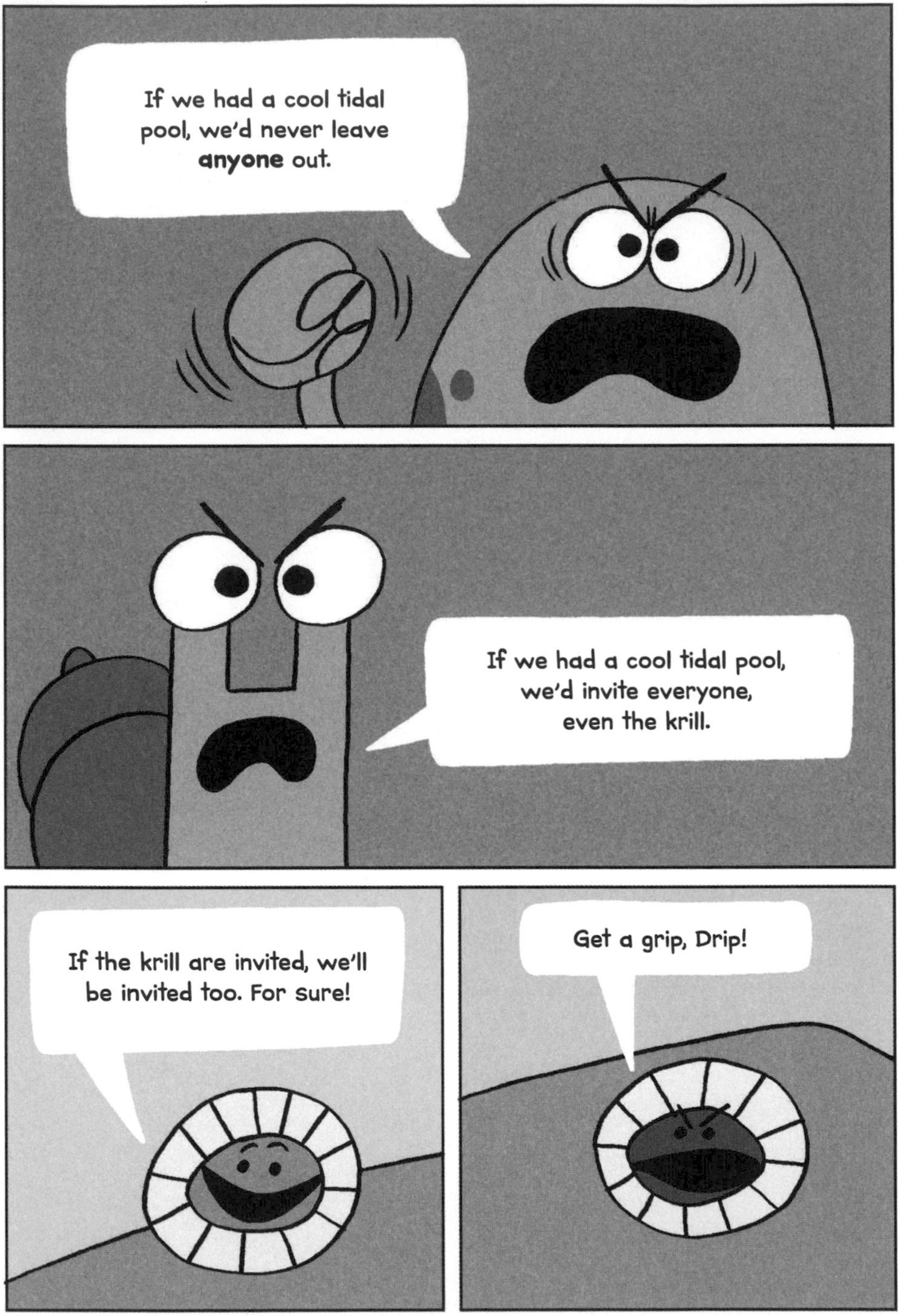
If we had a cool tidal pool, we'd never leave **anyone** out.
If we had a cool tidal pool, we'd invite everyone, even the krill.
If the krill are invited, we'll be invited too. For sure!
Get a grip, Drip!

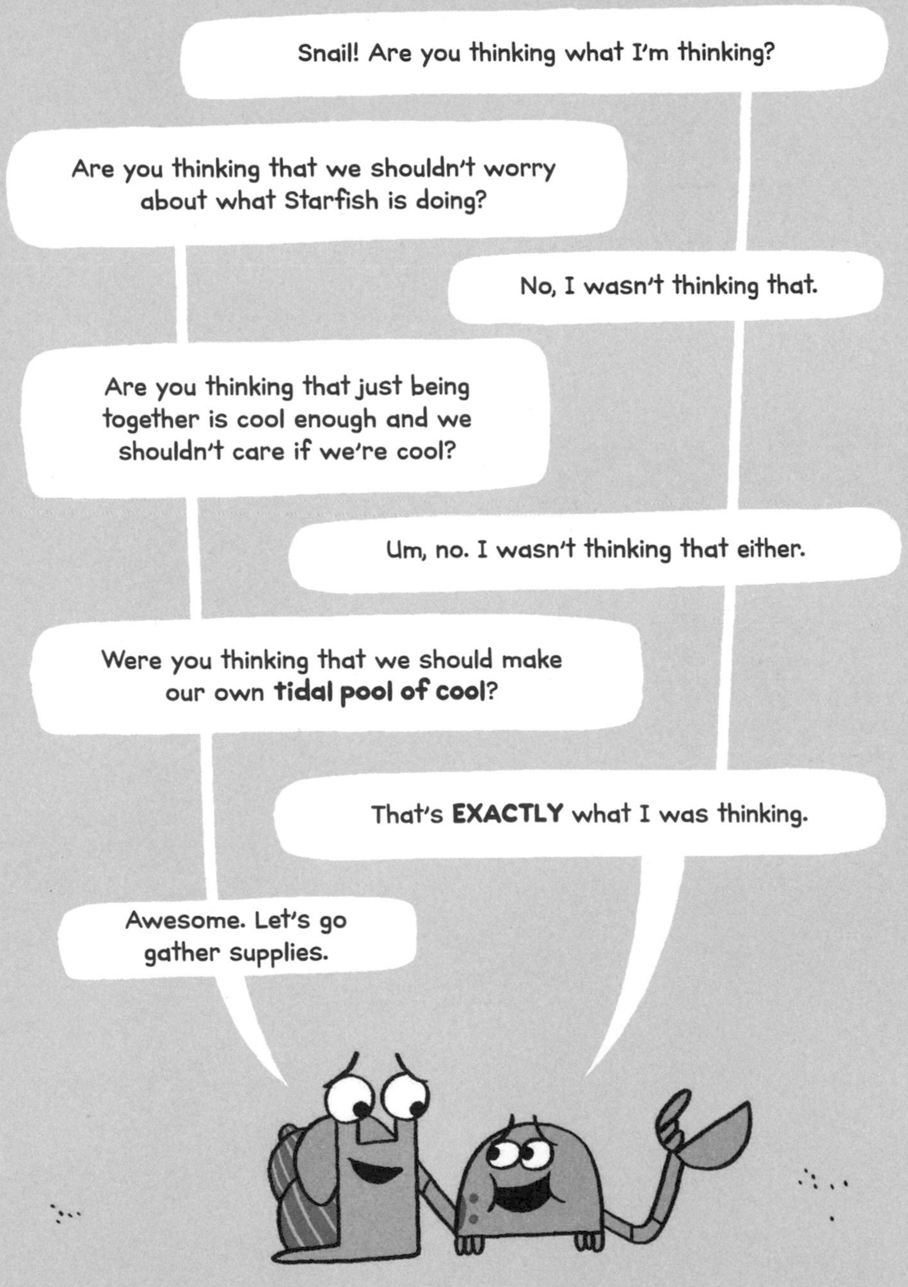
Snail! Are you thinking what I'm thinking?
Are you thinking that we shouldn't worry about what Starfish is doing?
No, I wasn't thinking that.
Are you thinking that just being together is cool enough and we shouldn't care if we're cool?
Um, no. I wasn't thinking that either.
Were you thinking that we should make our own **tidal pool of cool**?
That's **EXACTLY** what I was thinking.
Awesome. Let's go gather supplies.

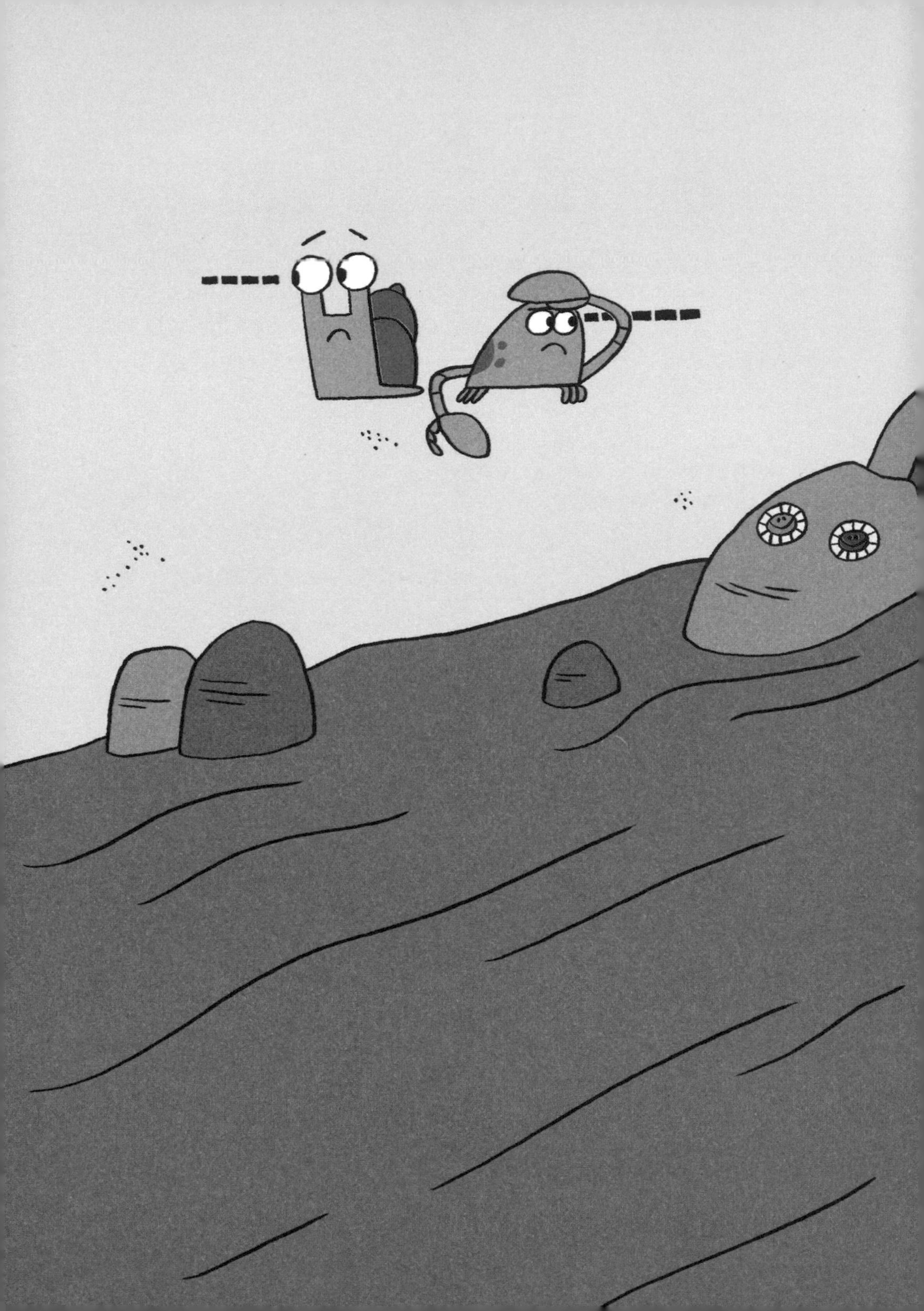

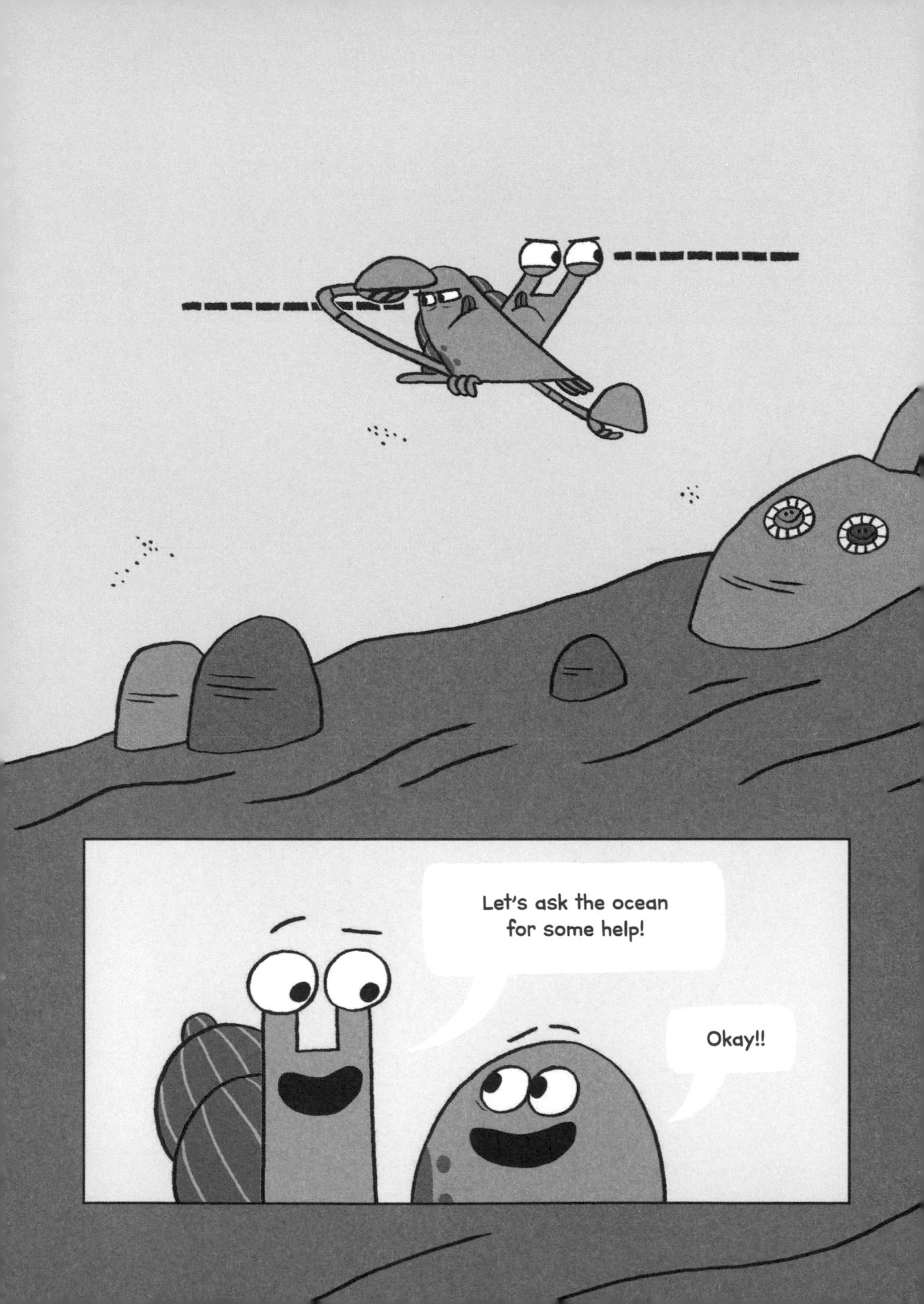
Let's ask the ocean for some help!
Okay!!

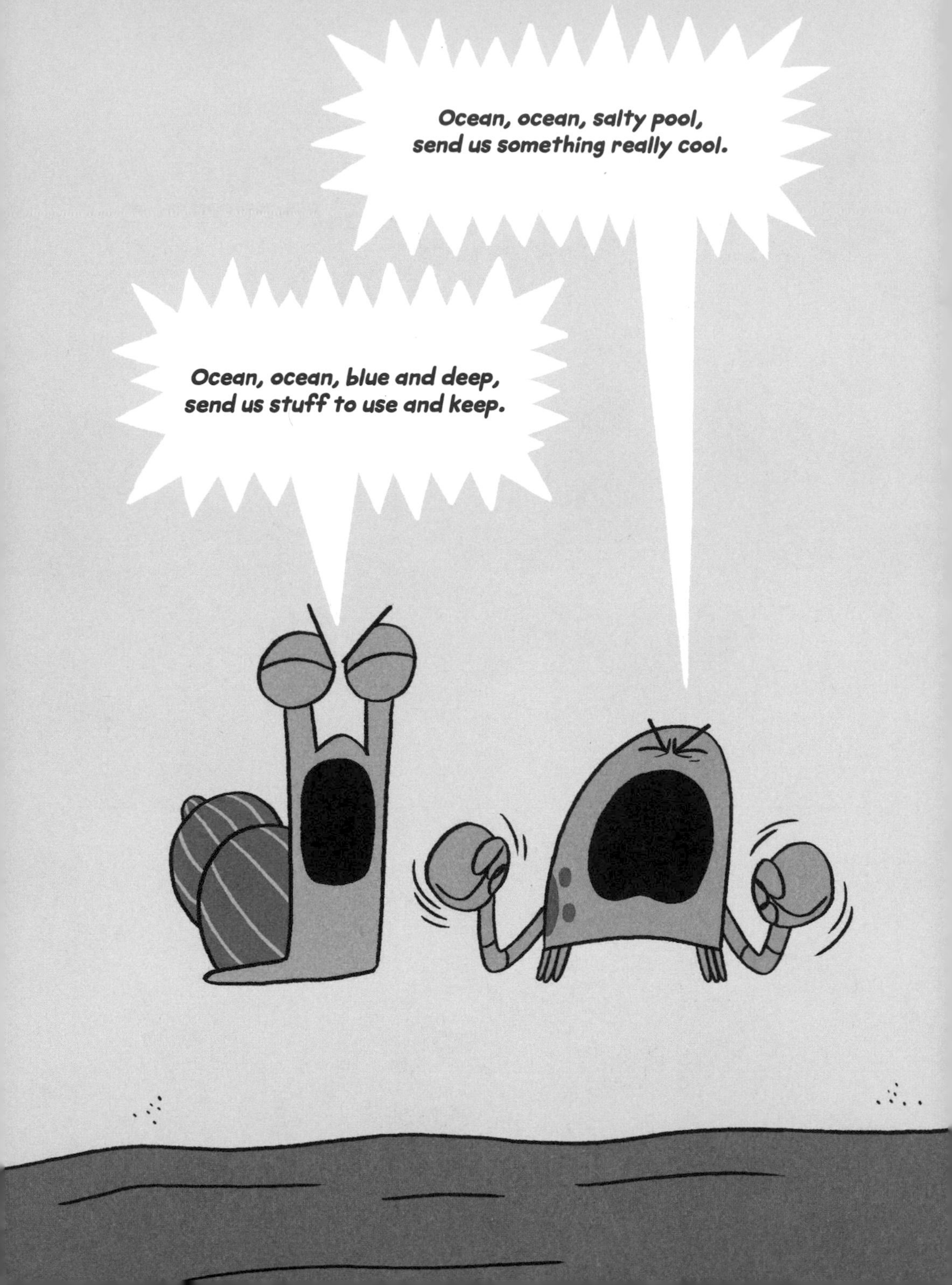
Ocean, ocean, salty pool, send us something really cool.
Ocean, ocean, blue and deep, send us stuff to use and keep.

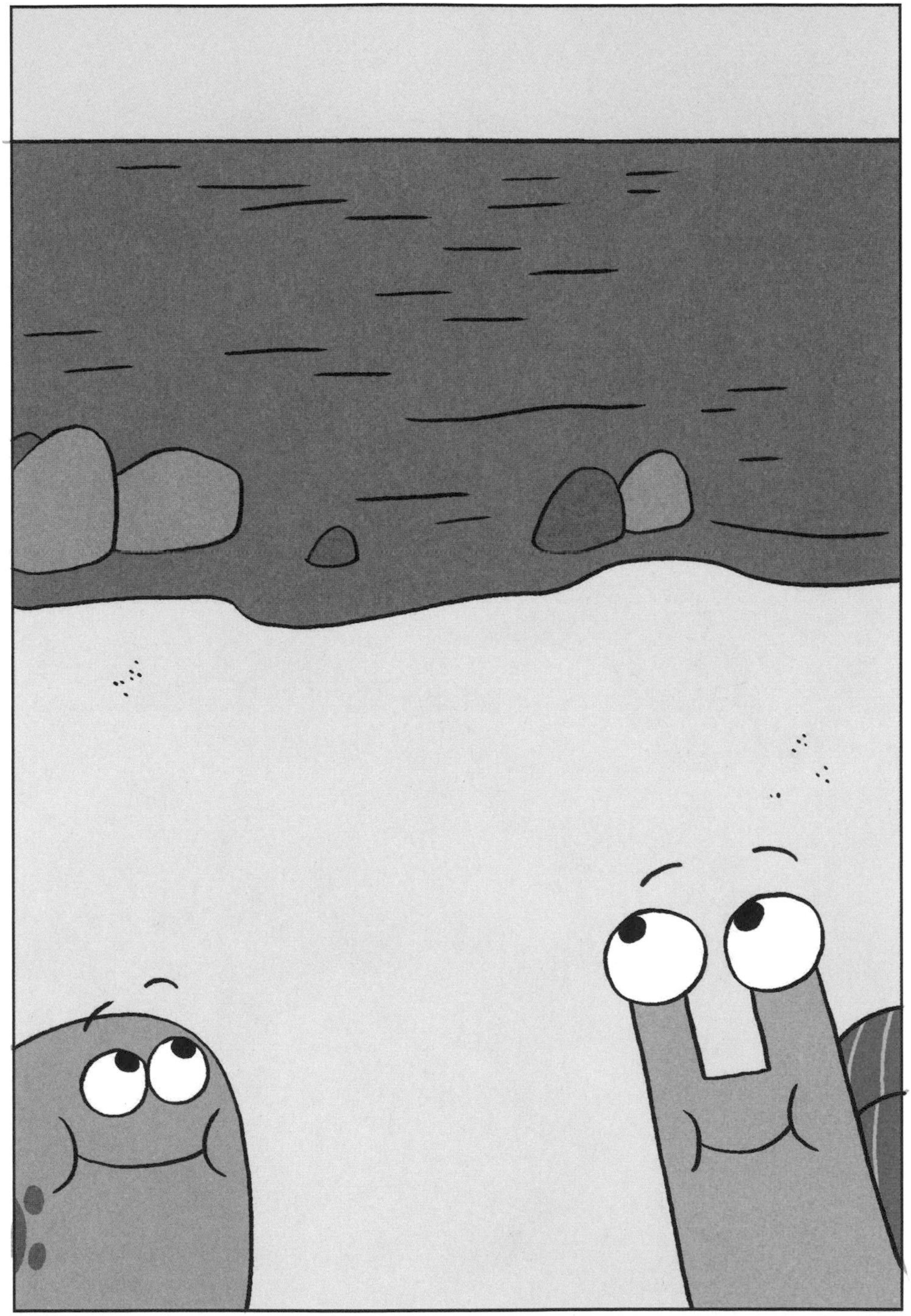

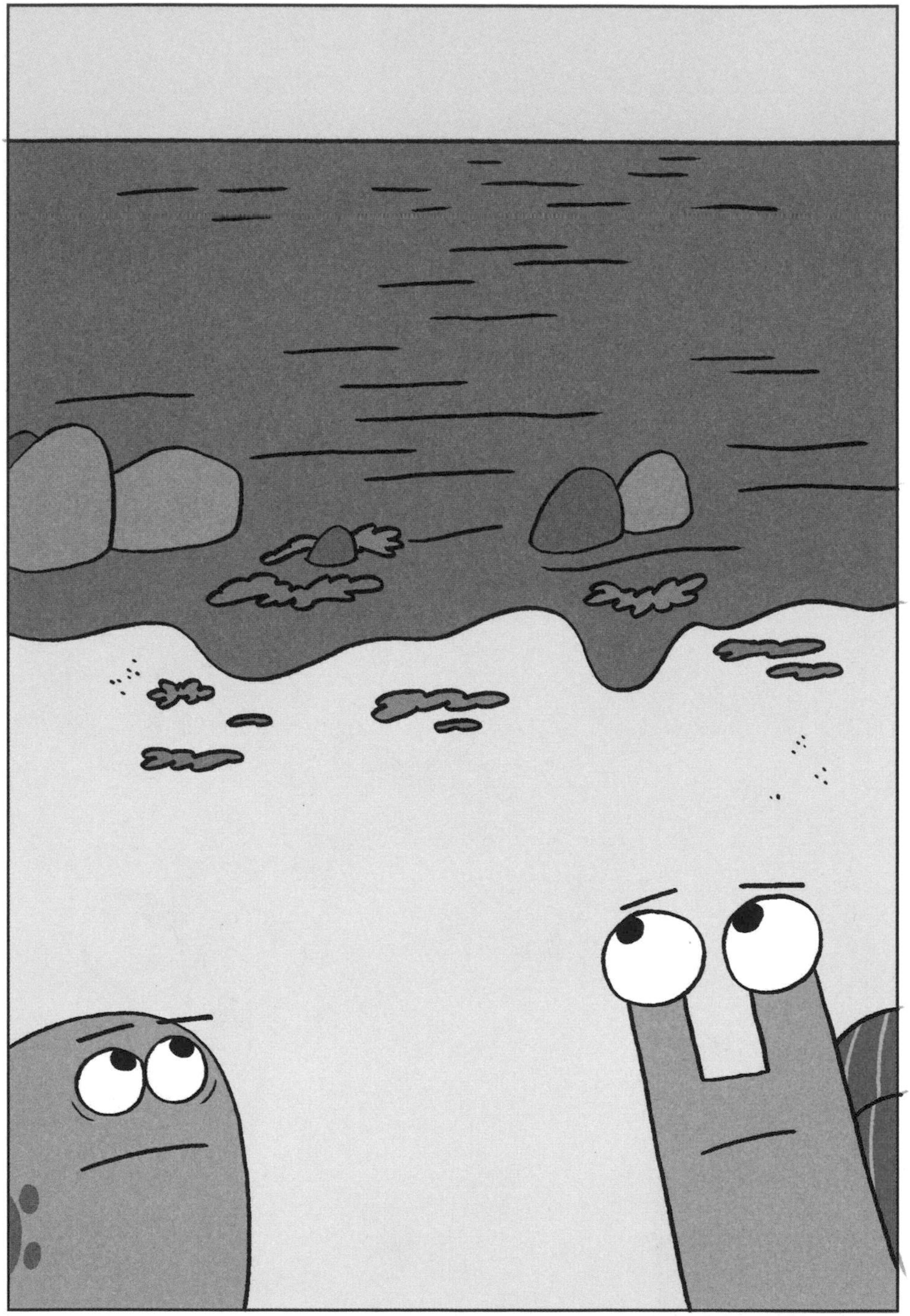

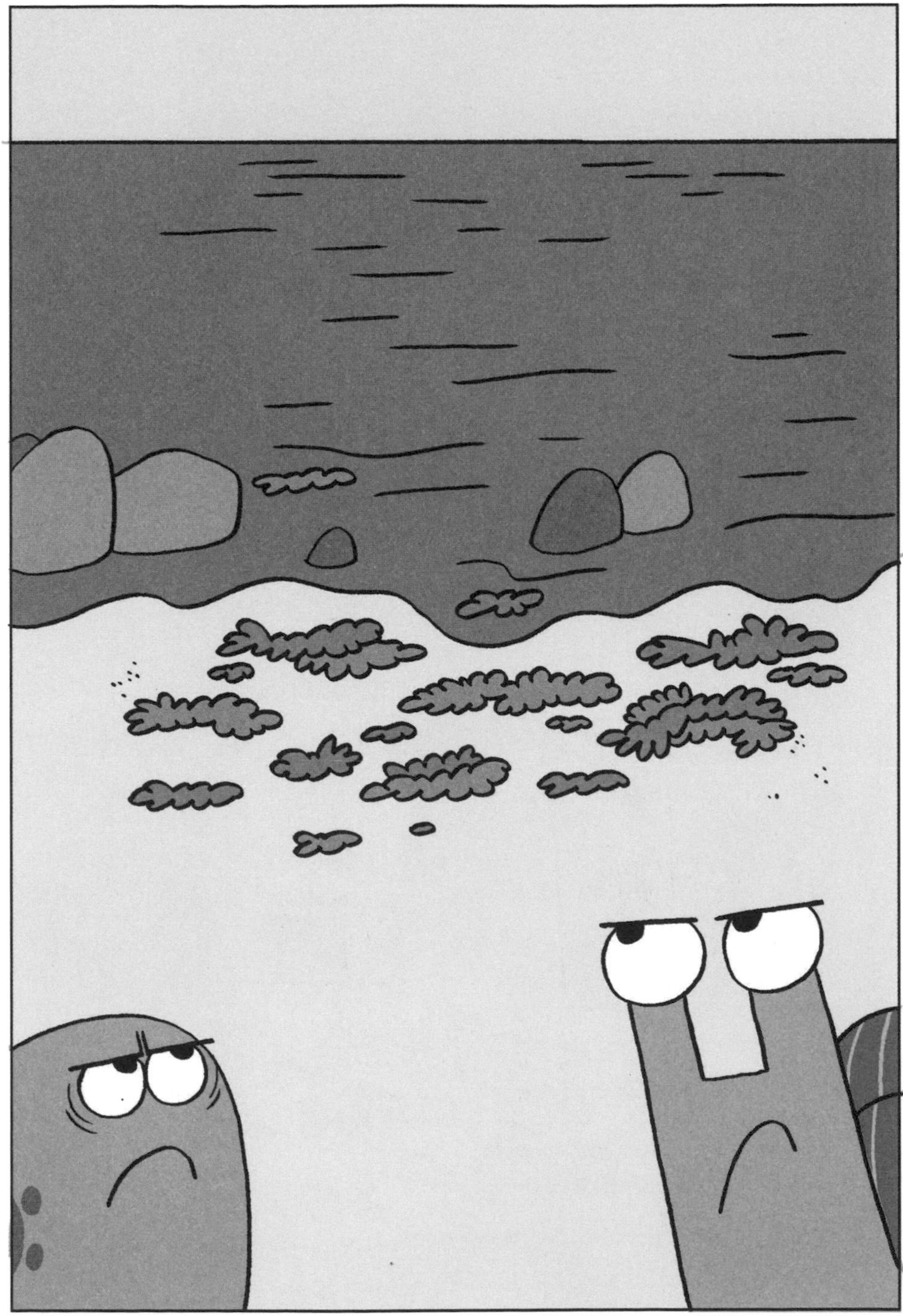

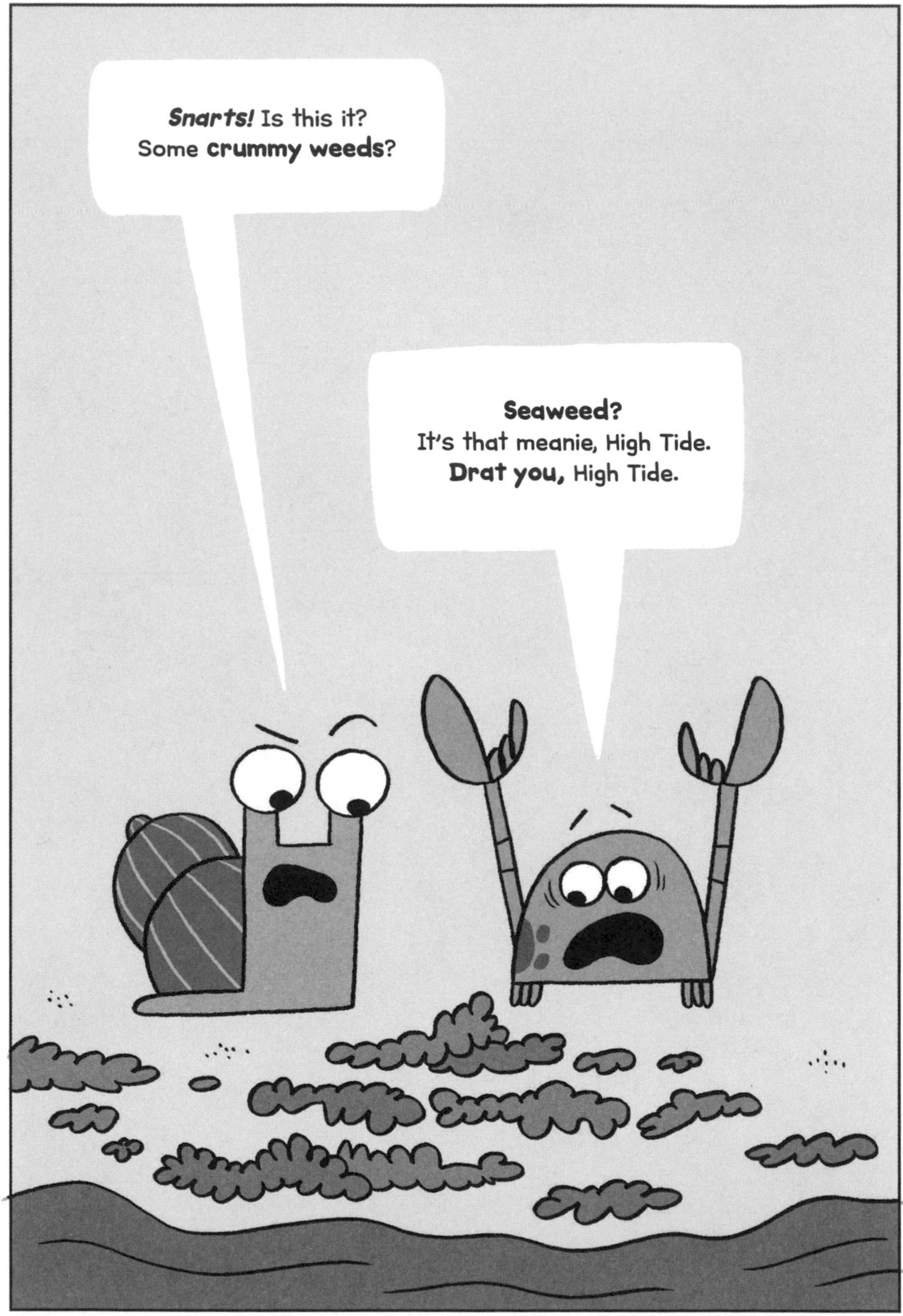
Snarts! Is this it? Some **crummy weeds**?
Seaweed? It's that meanie, High Tide. **Drat you,** High Tide.

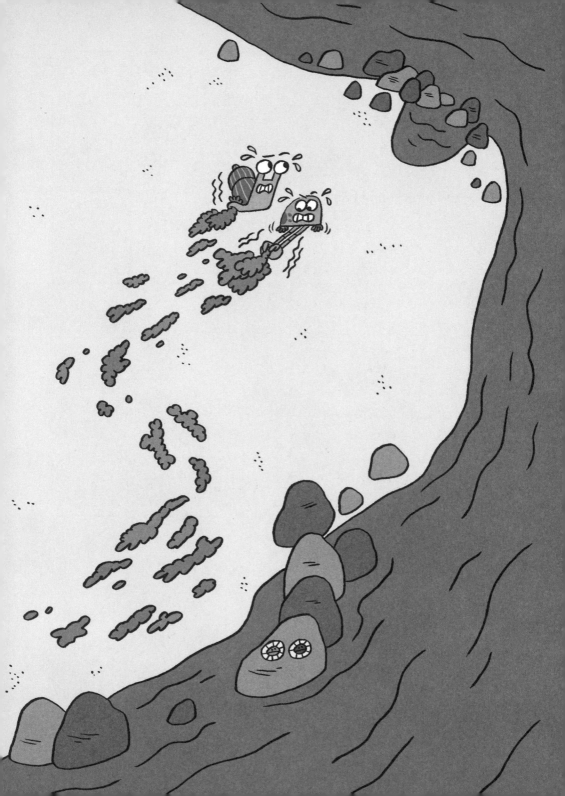

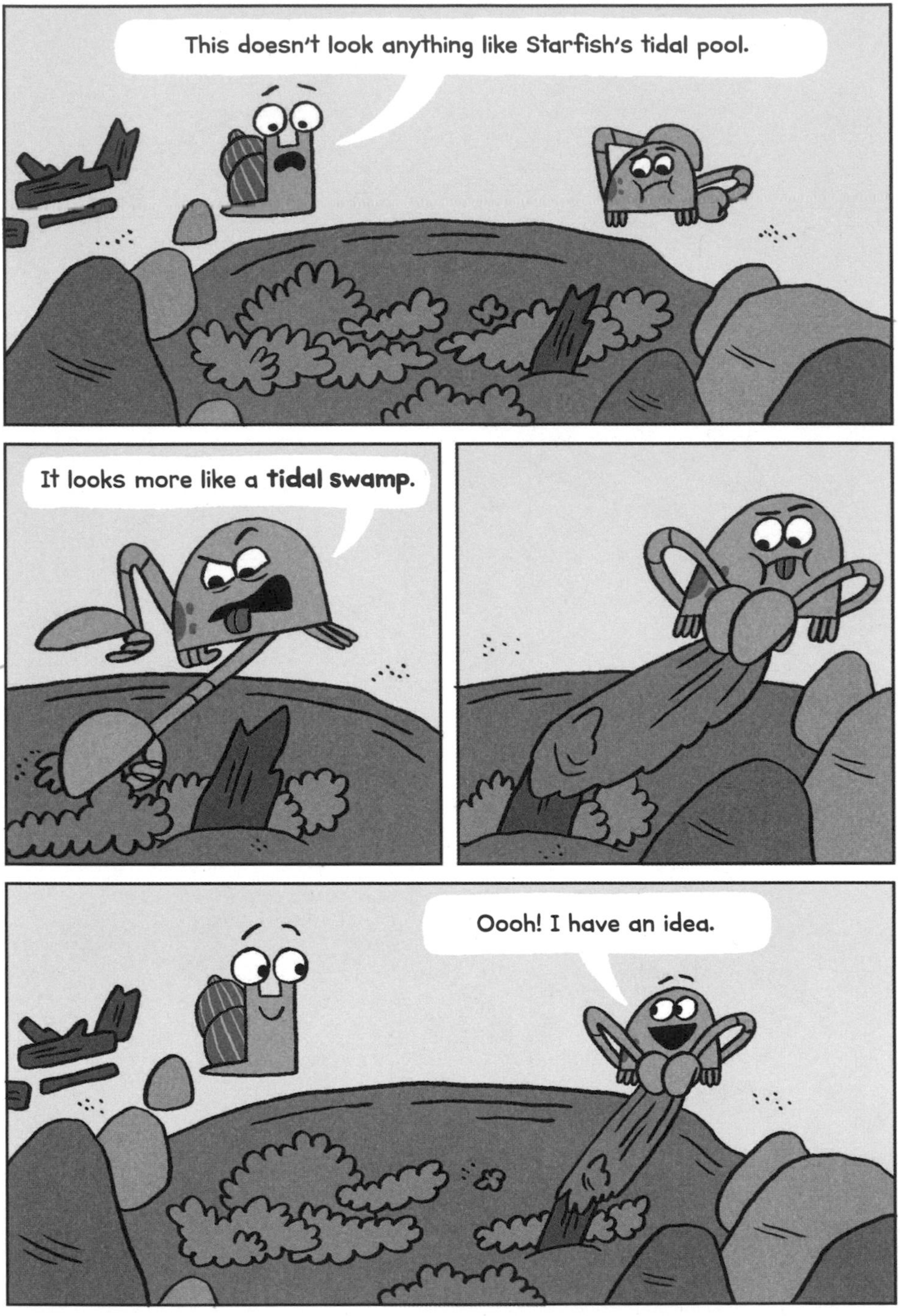
This doesn't look anything like Starfish's tidal pool.
It looks more like a **tidal swamp**.
Oooh! I have an idea.

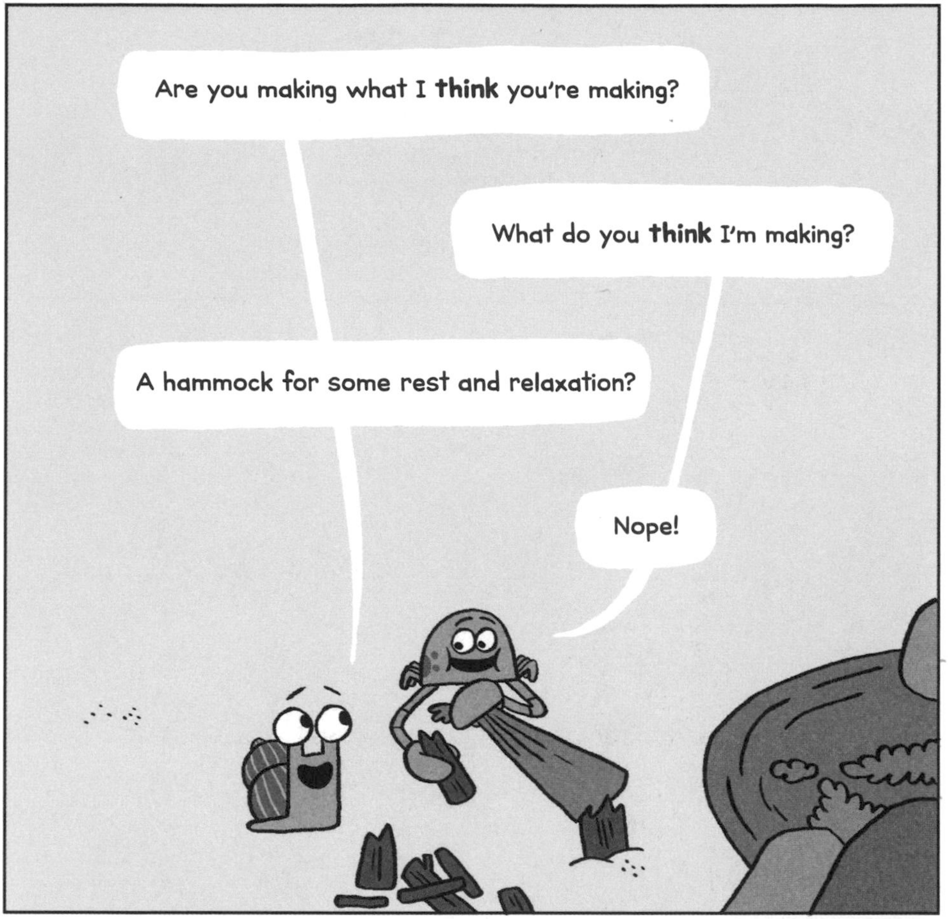
Are you making what I **think** you're making?
What do you **think** I'm making?
A hammock for some rest and relaxation?
Nope!

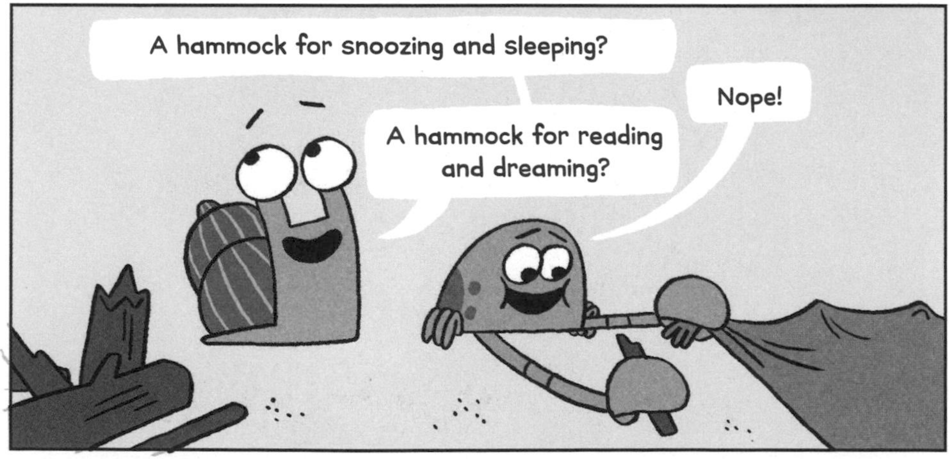
A hammock for snoozing and sleeping?
Nope!
A hammock for reading and dreaming?

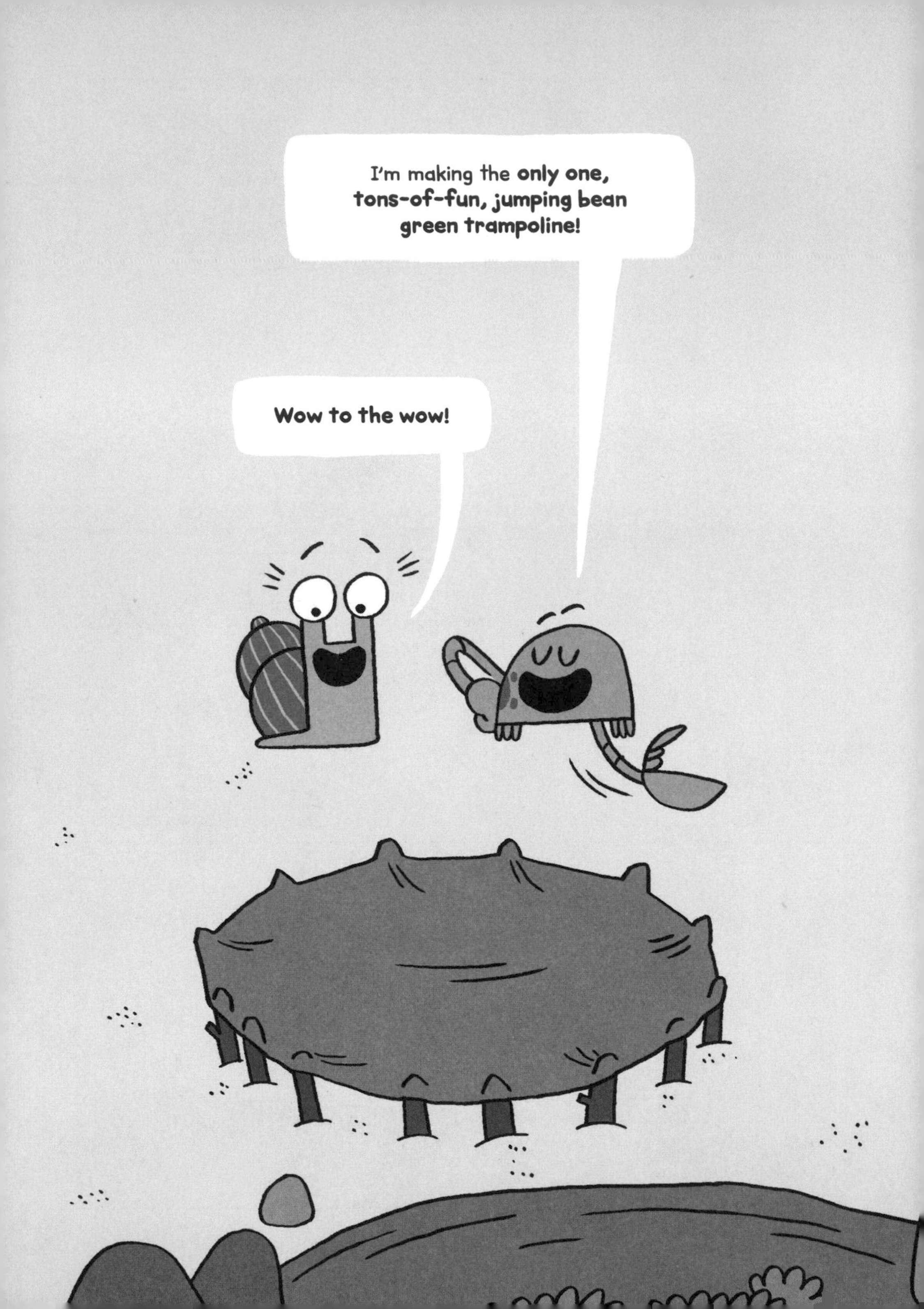
I'm making the **only one, tons-of-fun, jumping bean green trampoline!**
Wow to the wow!

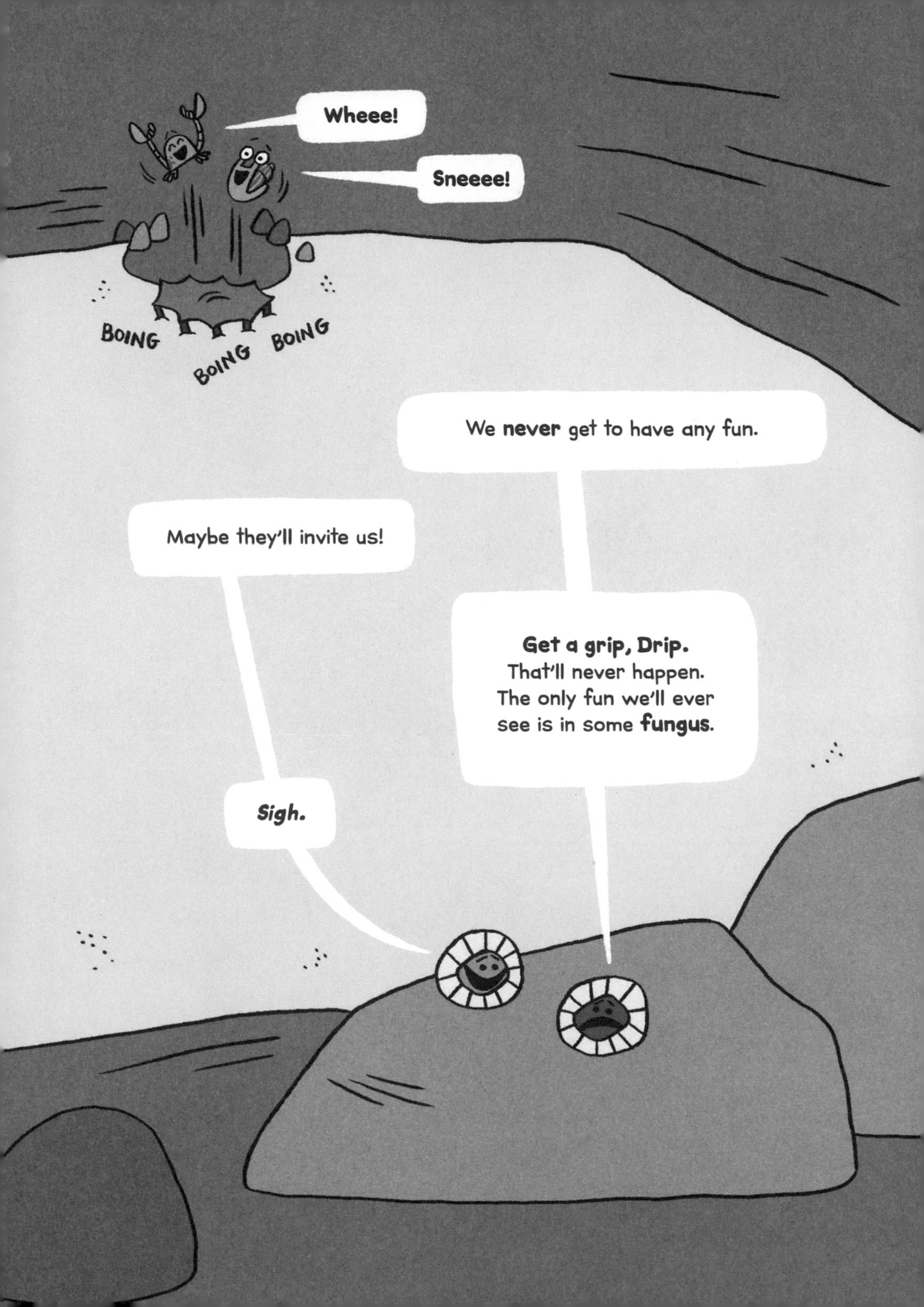
Wheee!
Sneeee!
BOING
BOING
BOING
We **never** get to have any fun.
Maybe they'll invite us!
Get a grip, Drip. That'll never happen. The only fun we'll ever see is in some **fungus**.
Sigh.

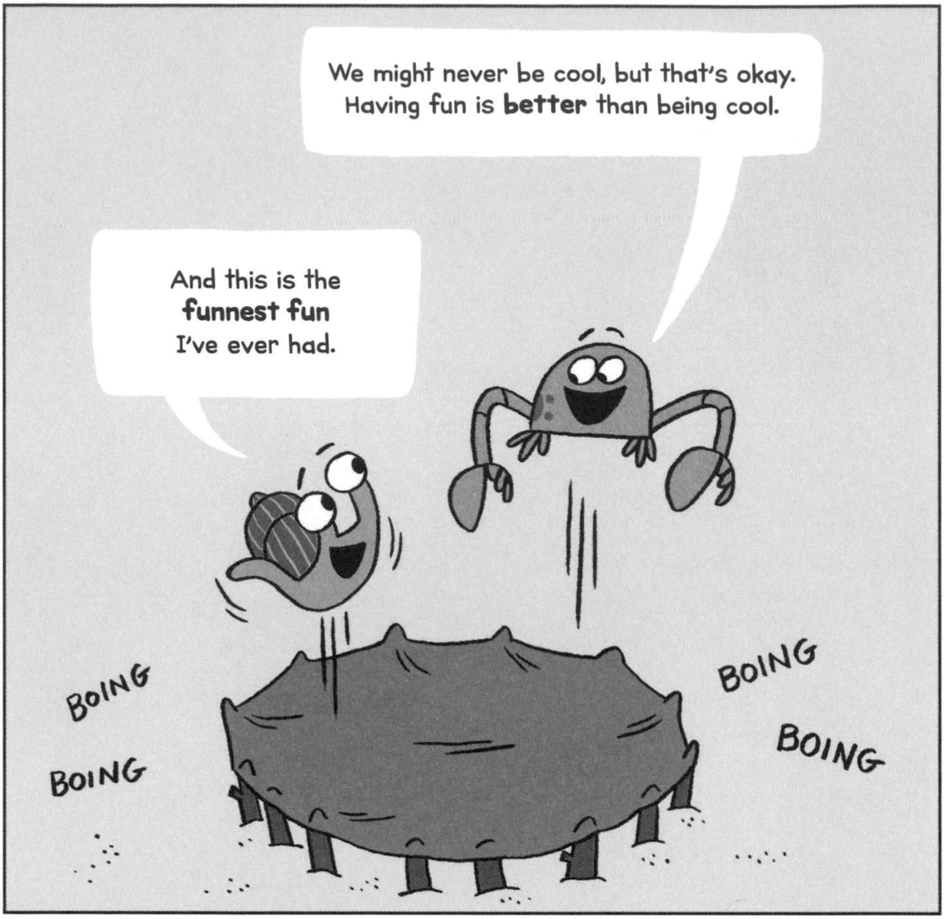
We might never be cool, but that's okay. Having fun is **better** than being cool.
And this is the **funnest fun** I've ever had.
BOING
BOING
BOING
BOING

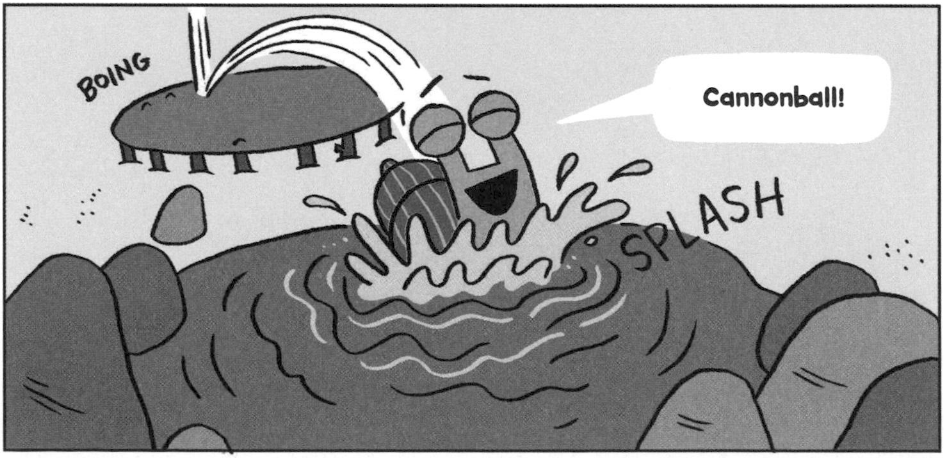
BOING
Cannonball!
SPLASH

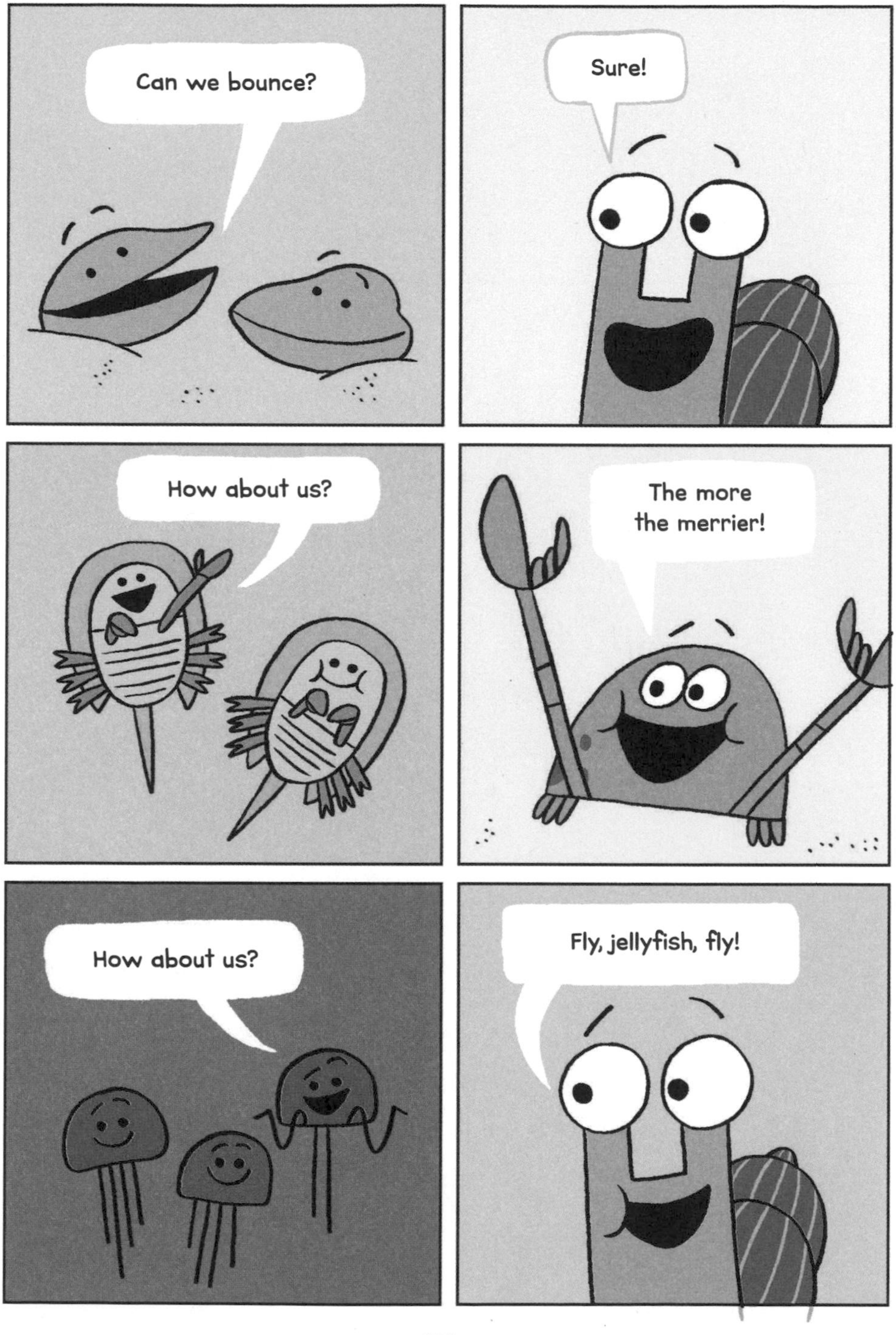
Can we bounce?
Sure!
How about us?
The more the merrier!
How about us?
Fly, jellyfish, fly!

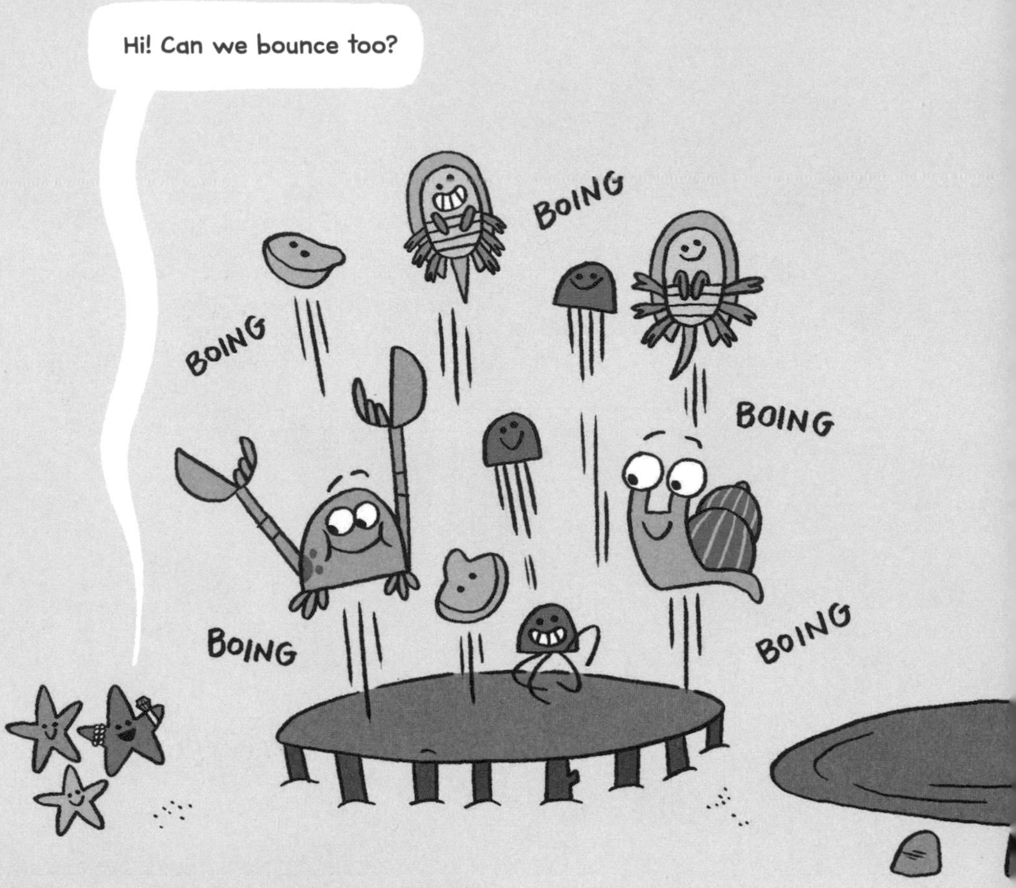
Hi! Can we bounce too?
BOING
BOING
BOING
BOING
BOING

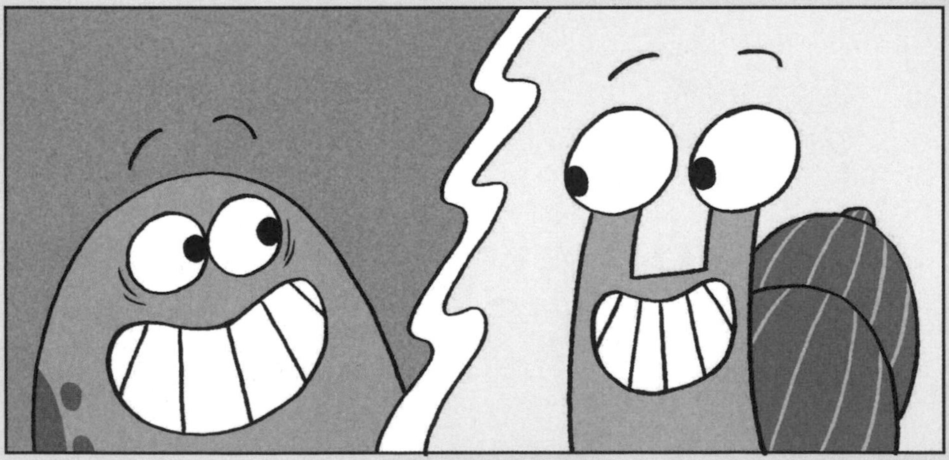

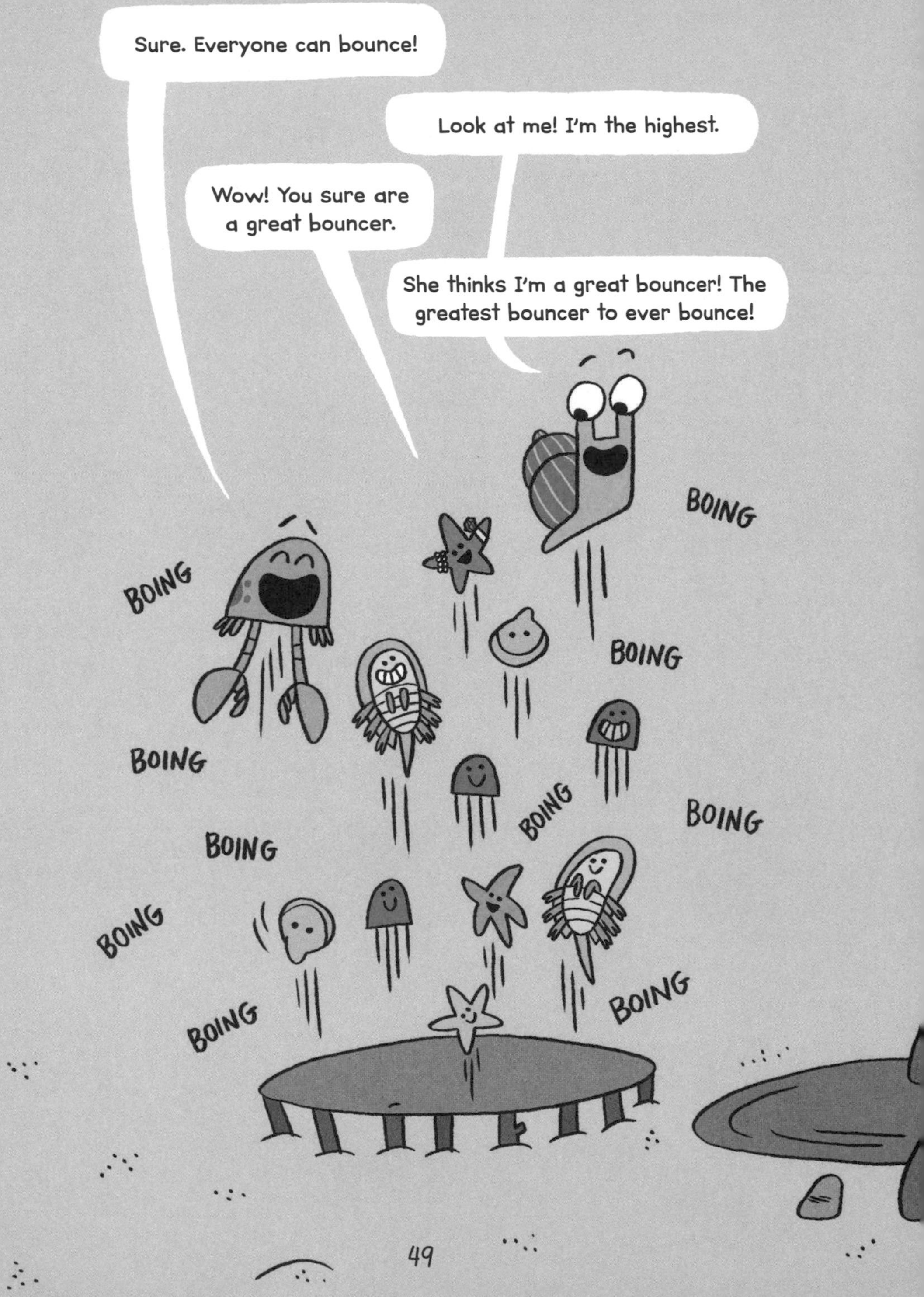
Sure. Everyone can bounce!
Look at me! I'm the highest.
Wow! You sure are a great bouncer.
She thinks I'm a great bouncer! The greatest bouncer to ever bounce!
BOING
BOING
BOING
BOING
BOING
BOING
BOING
BOING
BOING
BOING

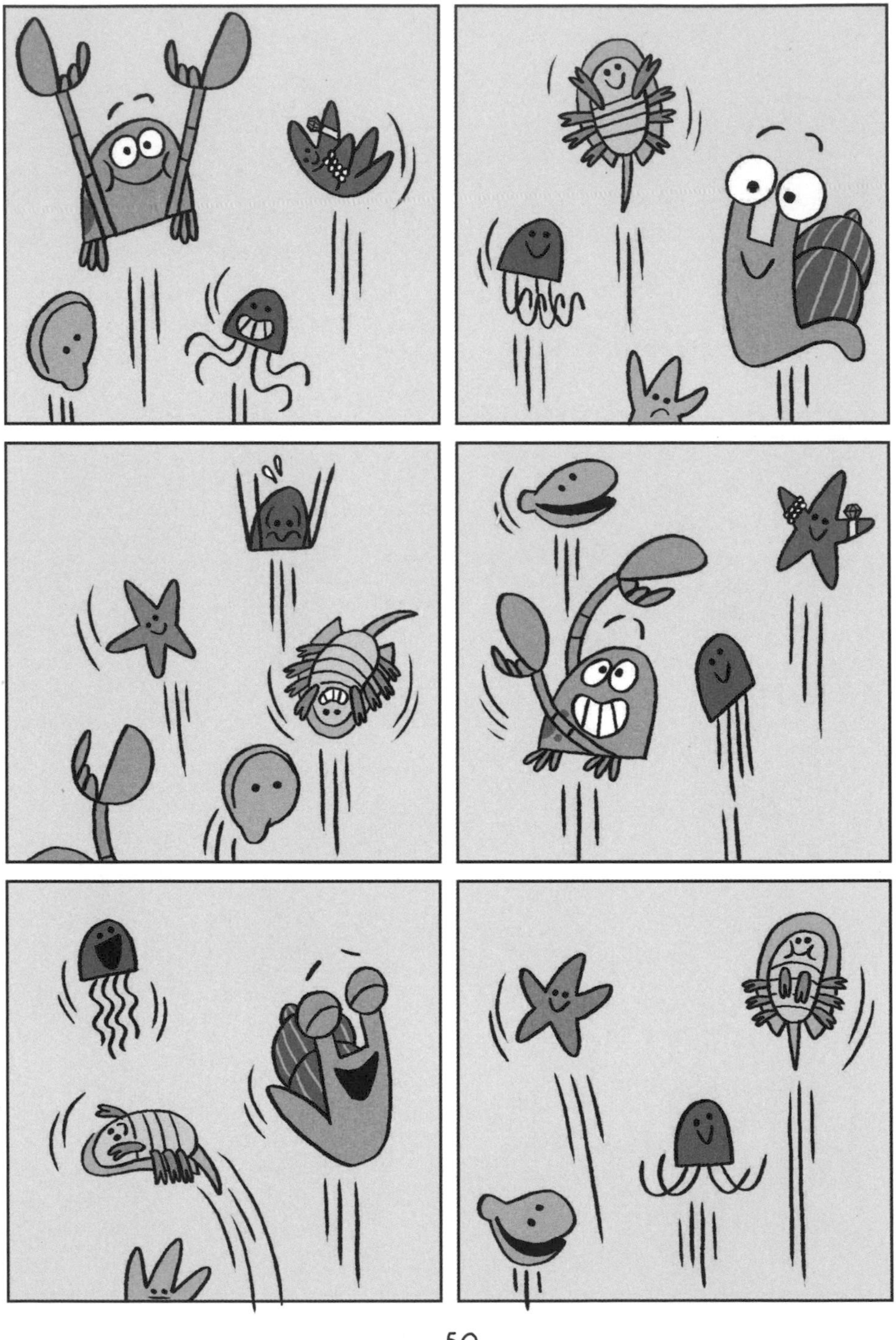

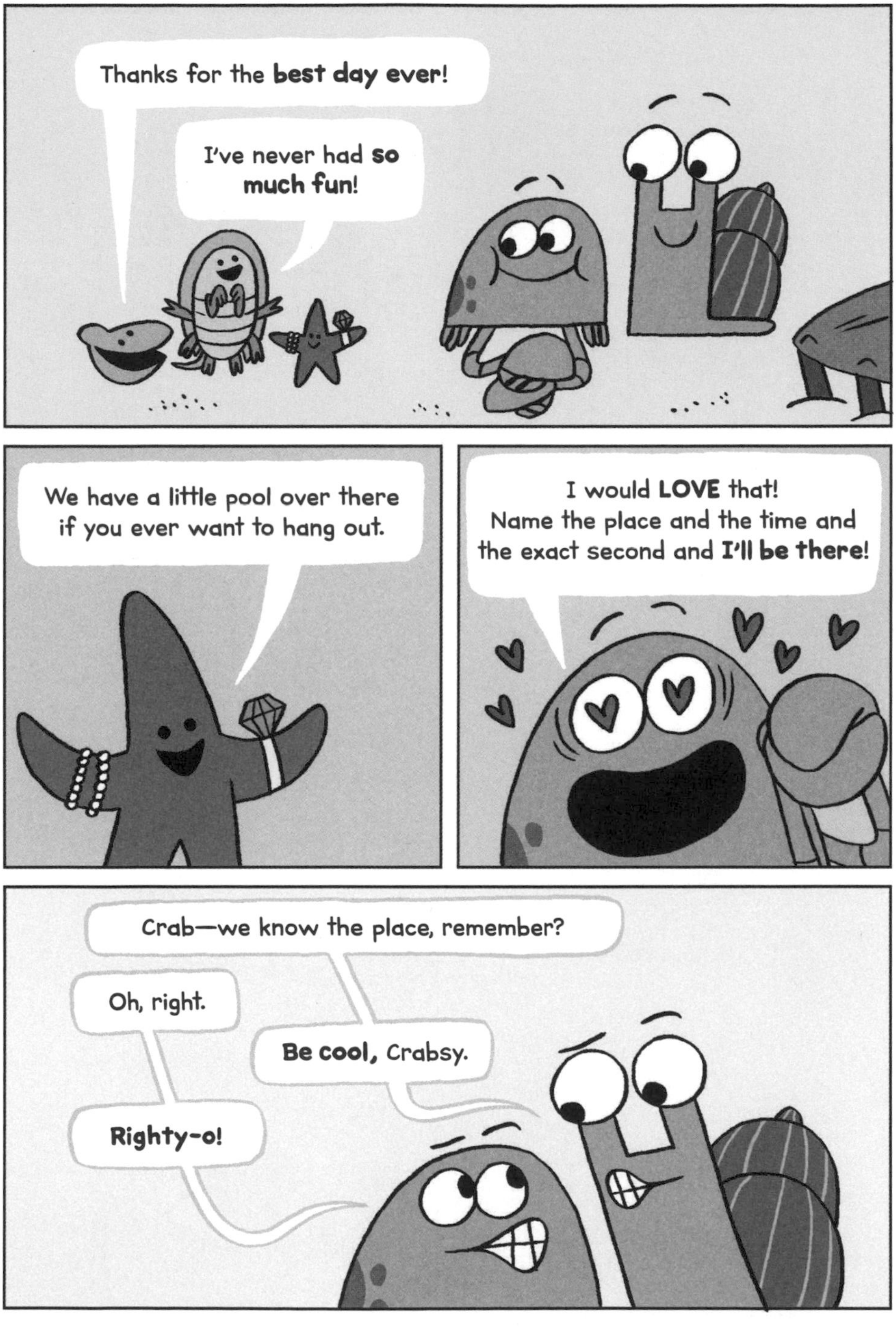
Thanks for the **best day ever**!
I've never had **so much fun**!
We have a little pool over there if you ever want to hang out.
I would **LOVE** that! Name the place and the time and the exact second and **I'll be there**!
Crab—we know the place, remember?
Oh, right.
Be cool, Crabsy.
Righty-o!

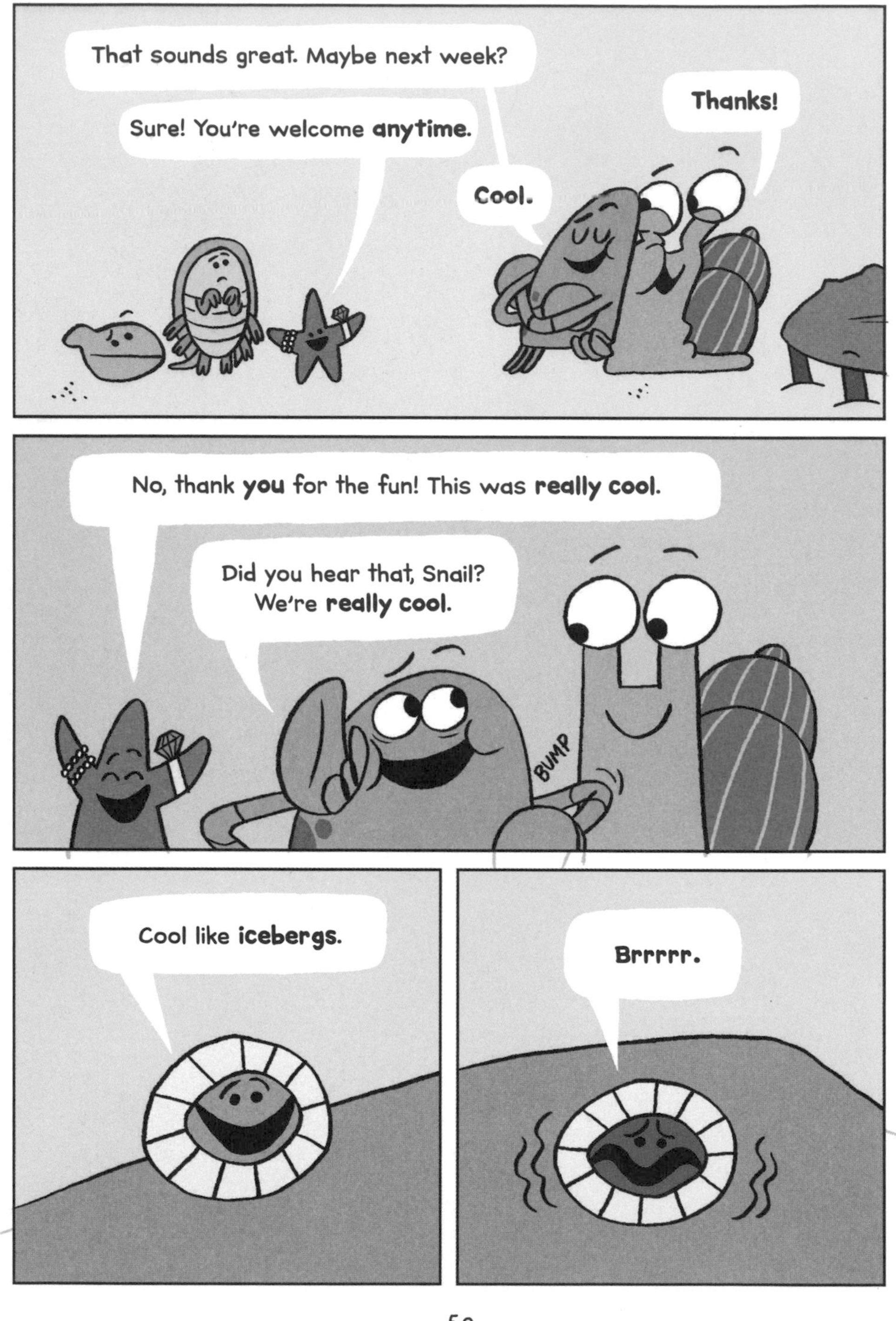
That sounds great. Maybe next week?
Sure! You're welcome **anytime**.
Cool.
Thanks!
No, thank **you** for the fun! This was **really cool**.
Did you hear that, Snail? We're **really cool**.
BUMP
Cool like **icebergs**.
Brrrrr.

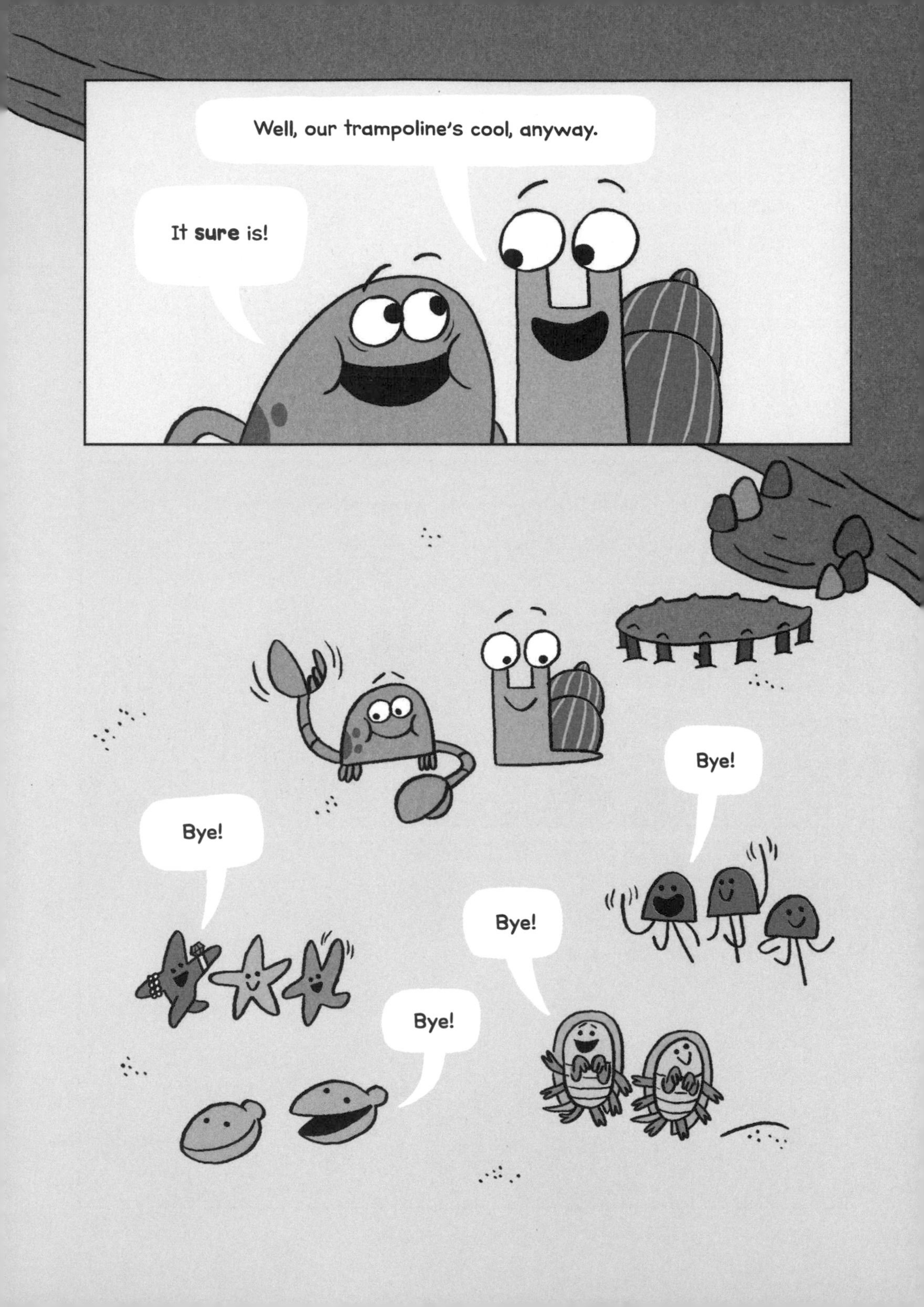
Well, our trampoline's cool, anyway.
It **sure** is!
Bye!
Bye!
Bye!
Bye!

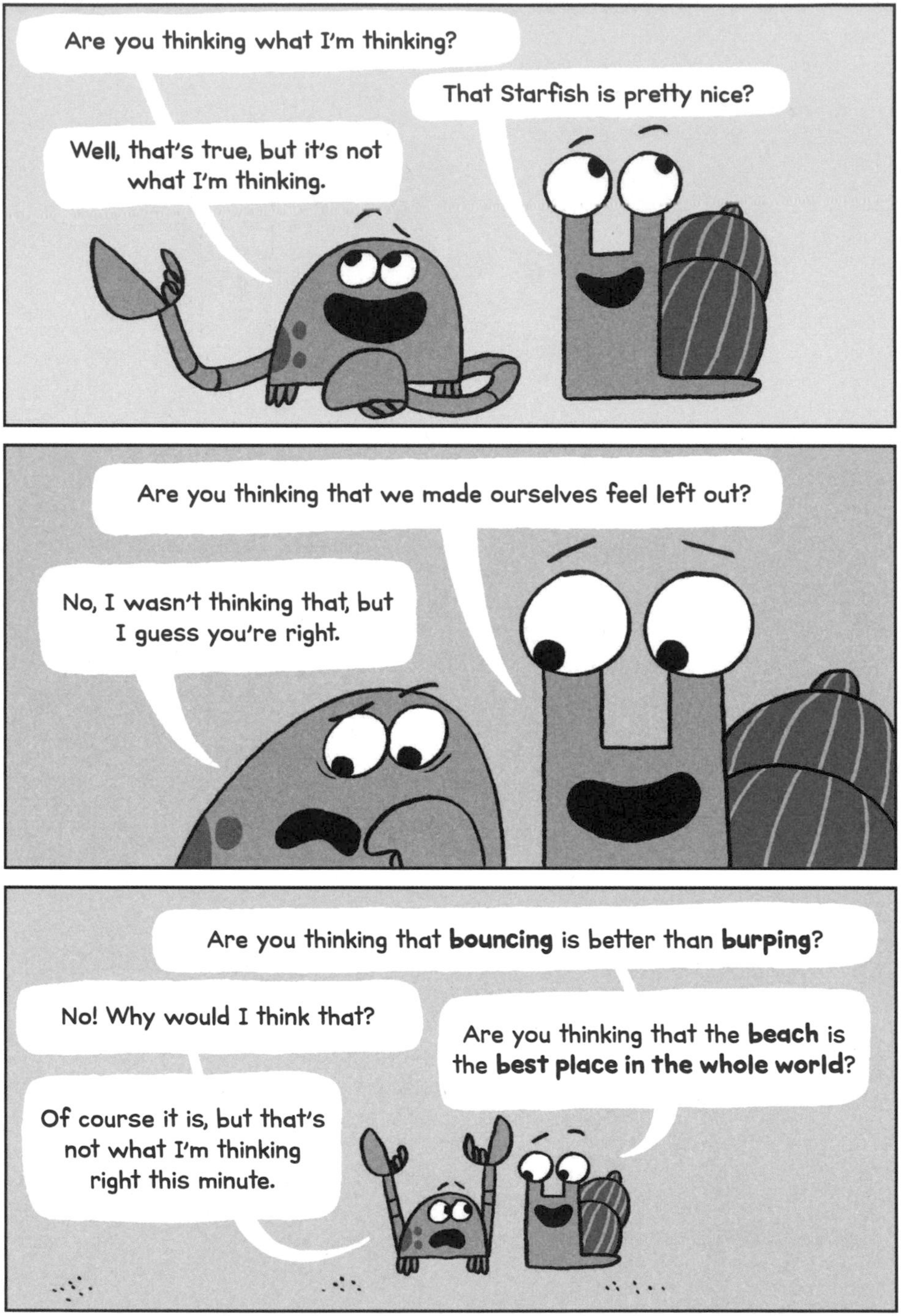
Are you thinking what I'm thinking?
That Starfish is pretty nice?
Well, that's true, but it's not what I'm thinking.
Are you thinking that we made ourselves feel left out?
No, I wasn't thinking that, but I guess you're right.
Are you thinking that **bouncing** is better than **burping**?
No! Why would I think that?
Are you thinking that the **beach** is the **best place in the whole world**?
Of course it is, but that's not what I'm thinking right this minute.

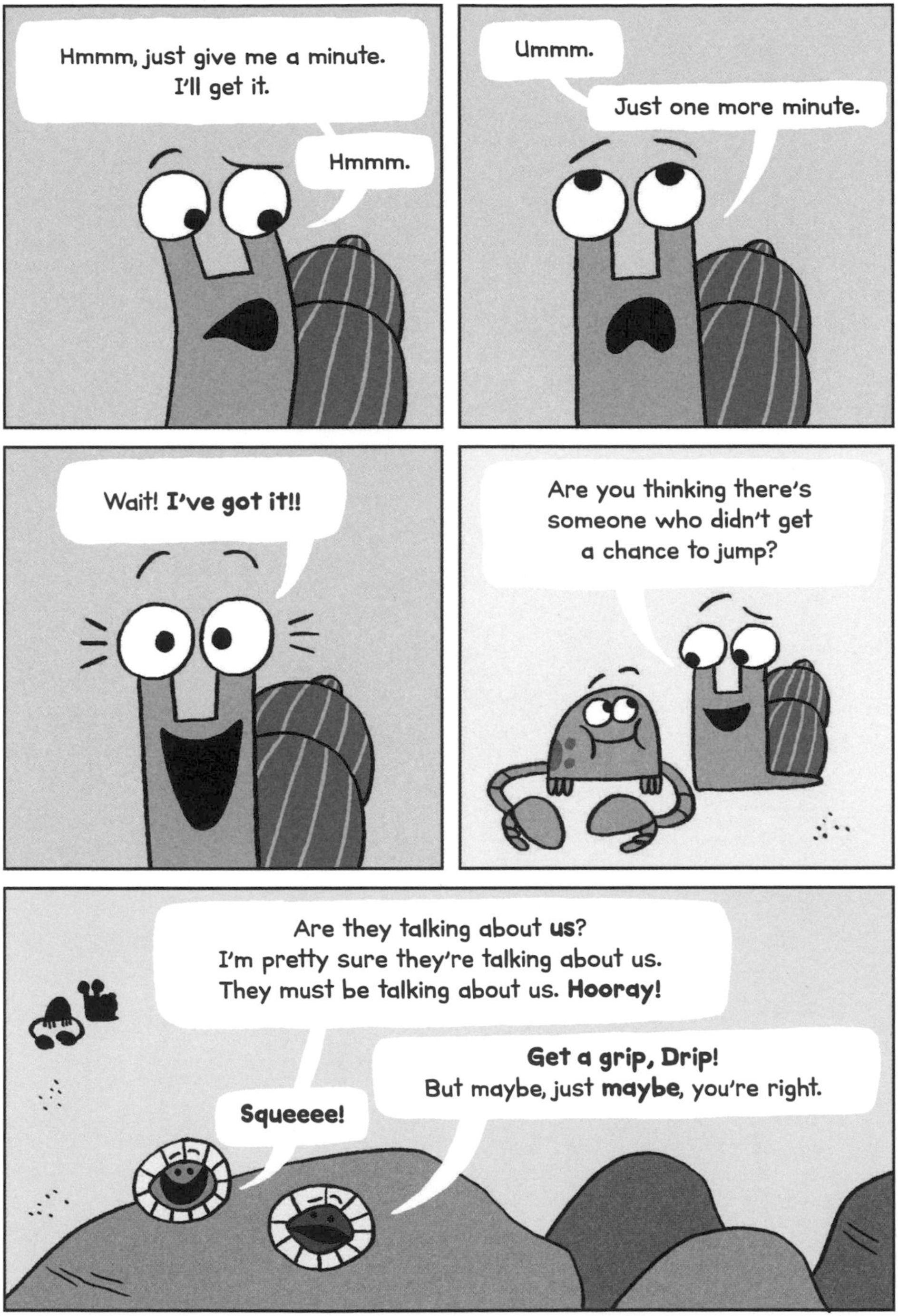
Hmmm, just give me a minute. I'll get it.
Hmmm.
Ummm.
Just one more minute.
Wait! I've got it!!
Are you thinking there's someone who didn't get a chance to jump?
Are they talking about us? I'm pretty sure they're talking about us. They must be talking about us. Hooray!
Squeeee!
Get a grip, Drip! But maybe, just maybe, you're right.

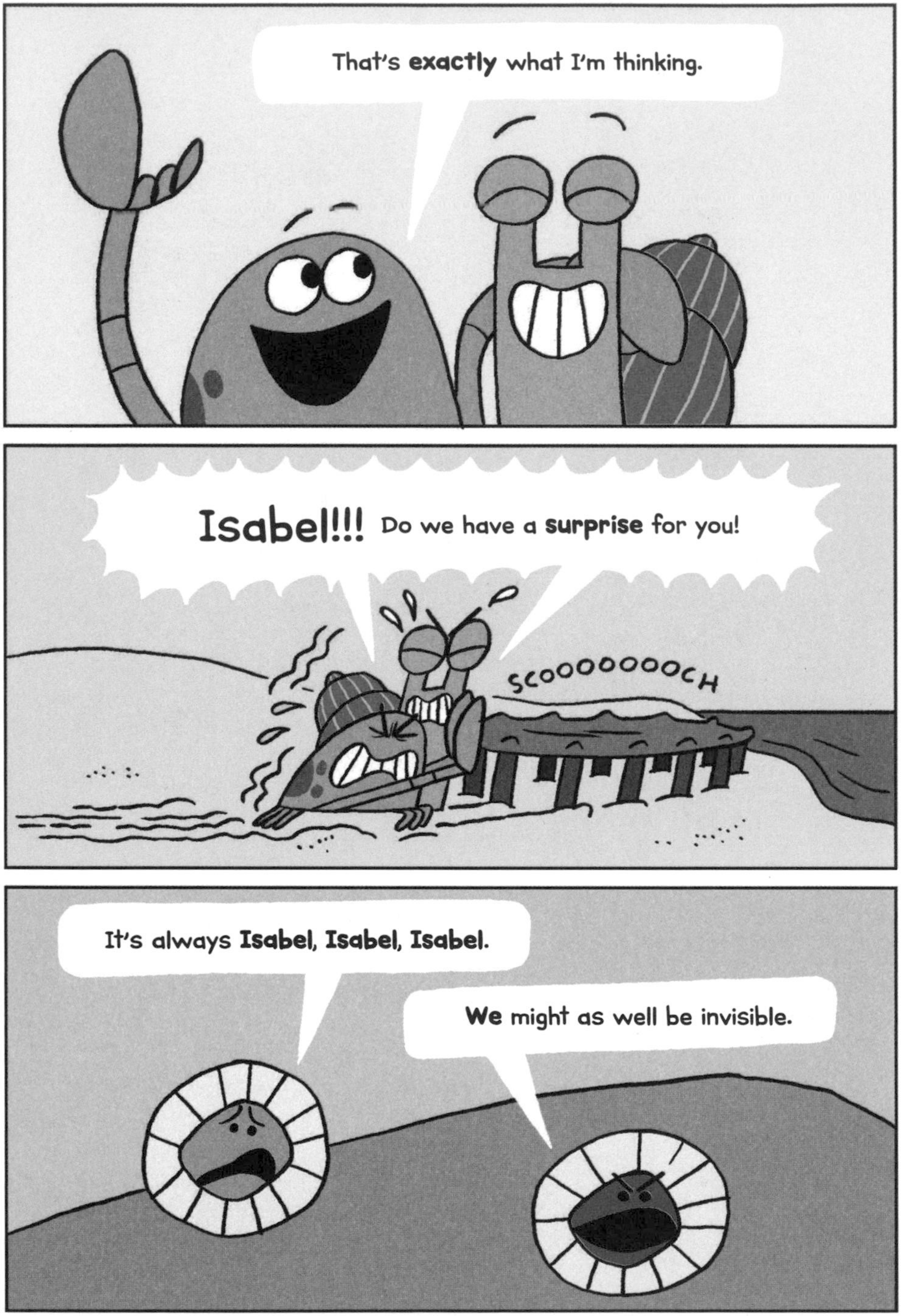
That's **exactly** what I'm thinking.
Isabel!!! Do we have a **surprise** for you!
SCOOOOOOOOCH
It's always **Isabel, Isabel, Isabel.**
We might as well be invisible.

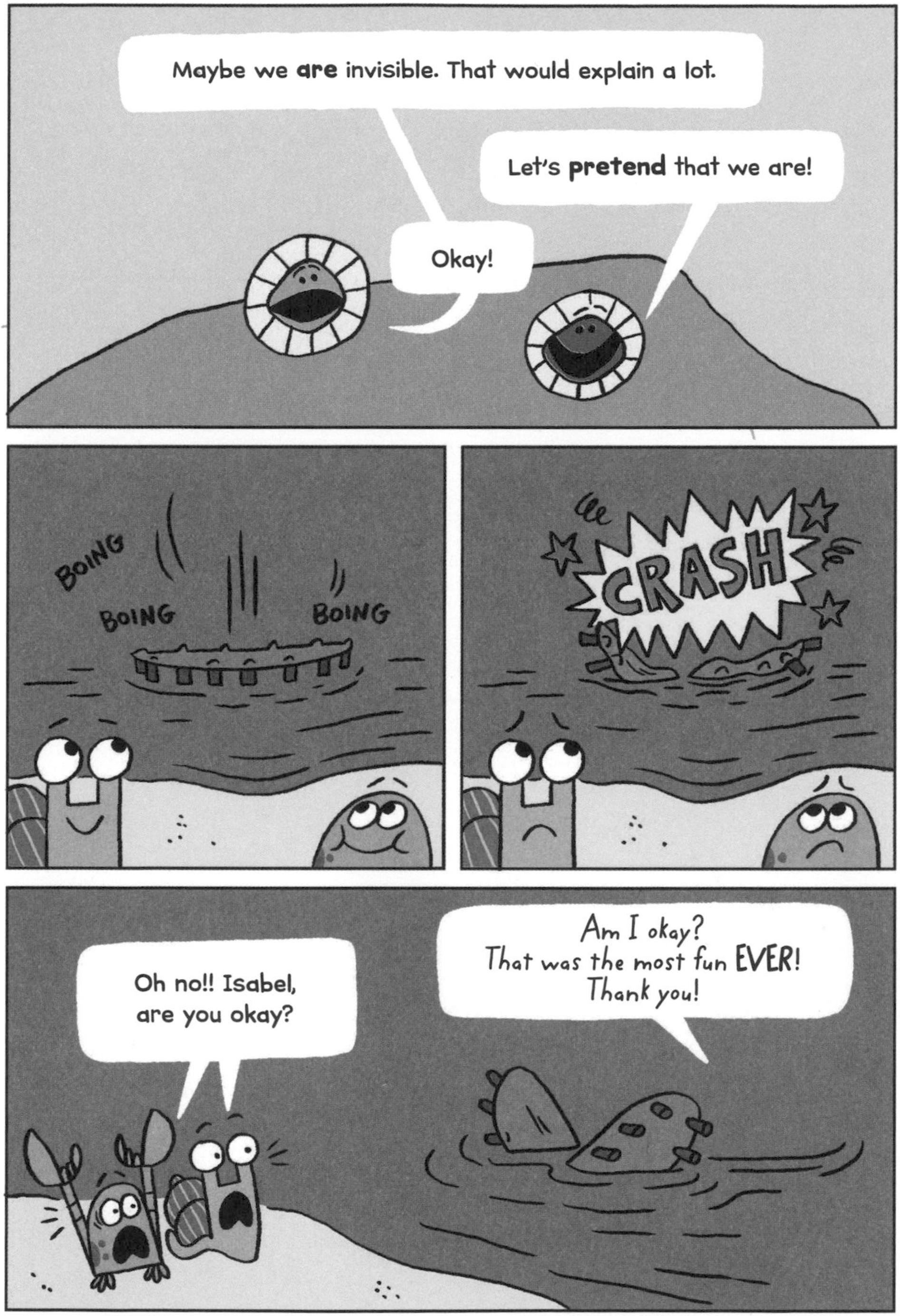
Maybe we **are** invisible. That would explain a lot.
Let's **pretend** that we are!
Okay!
BOING
BOING
BOING
CRASH
Oh no!! Isabel, are you okay?
Am I okay? That was the most fun **EVER**! Thank you!

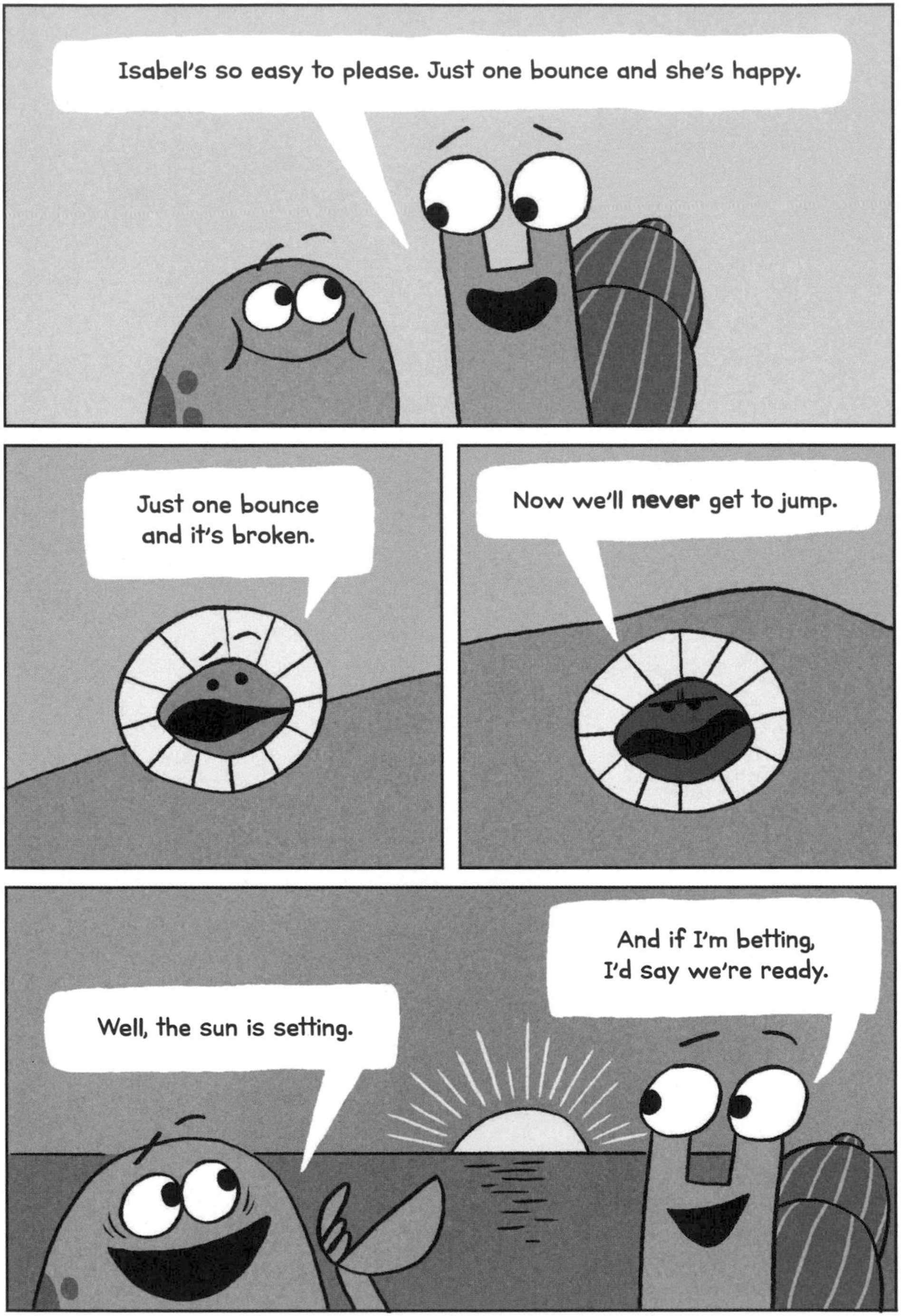
Isabel's so easy to please. Just one bounce and she's happy.
Just one bounce and it's broken.
Now we'll **never** get to jump.
Well, the sun is setting.
And if I'm betting, I'd say we're ready.

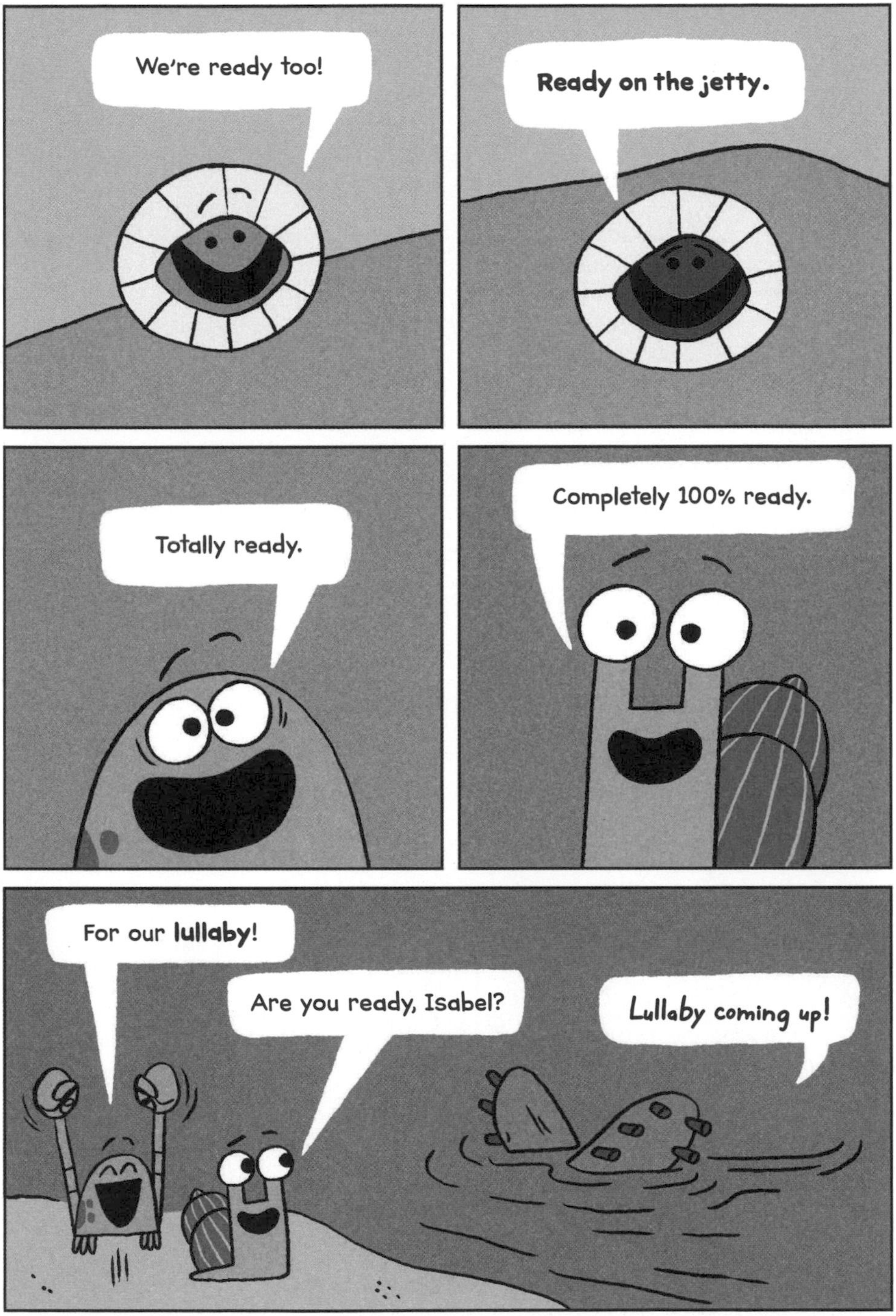
We're ready too!
Ready on the jetty.
Totally ready.
Completely 100% ready.
For our lullaby!
Are you ready, Isabel?
Lullaby coming up!

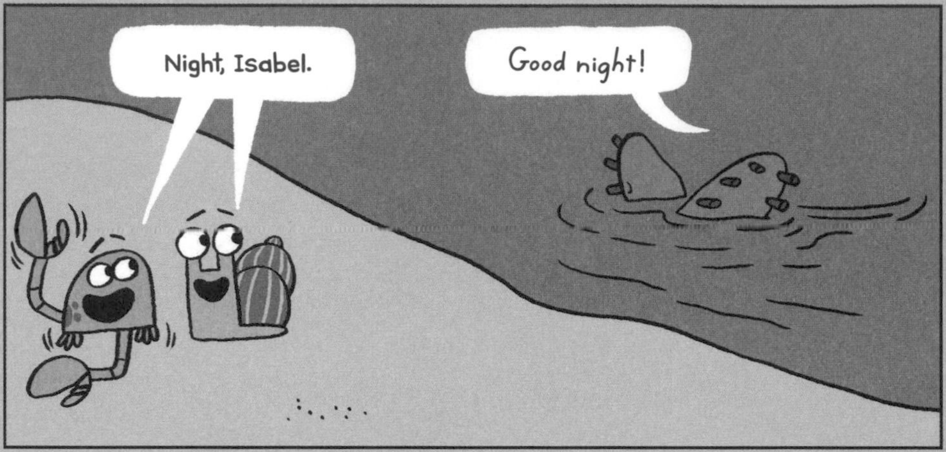
Night, Isabel.
Good night!

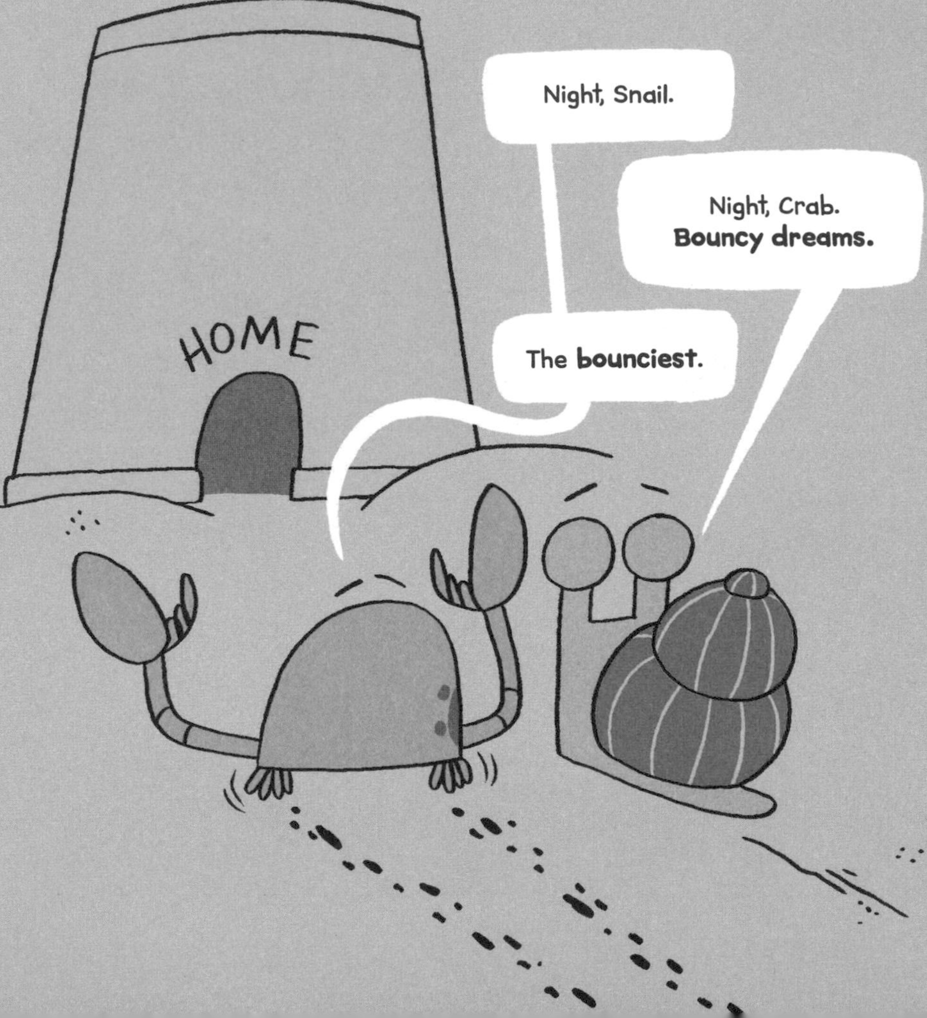
HOME
Night, Snail.
Night, Crab.
Bouncy dreams.
The **bounciest**.

Well, at least we can bounce in our dreams.
Bounce, barnacle brother, bounce!

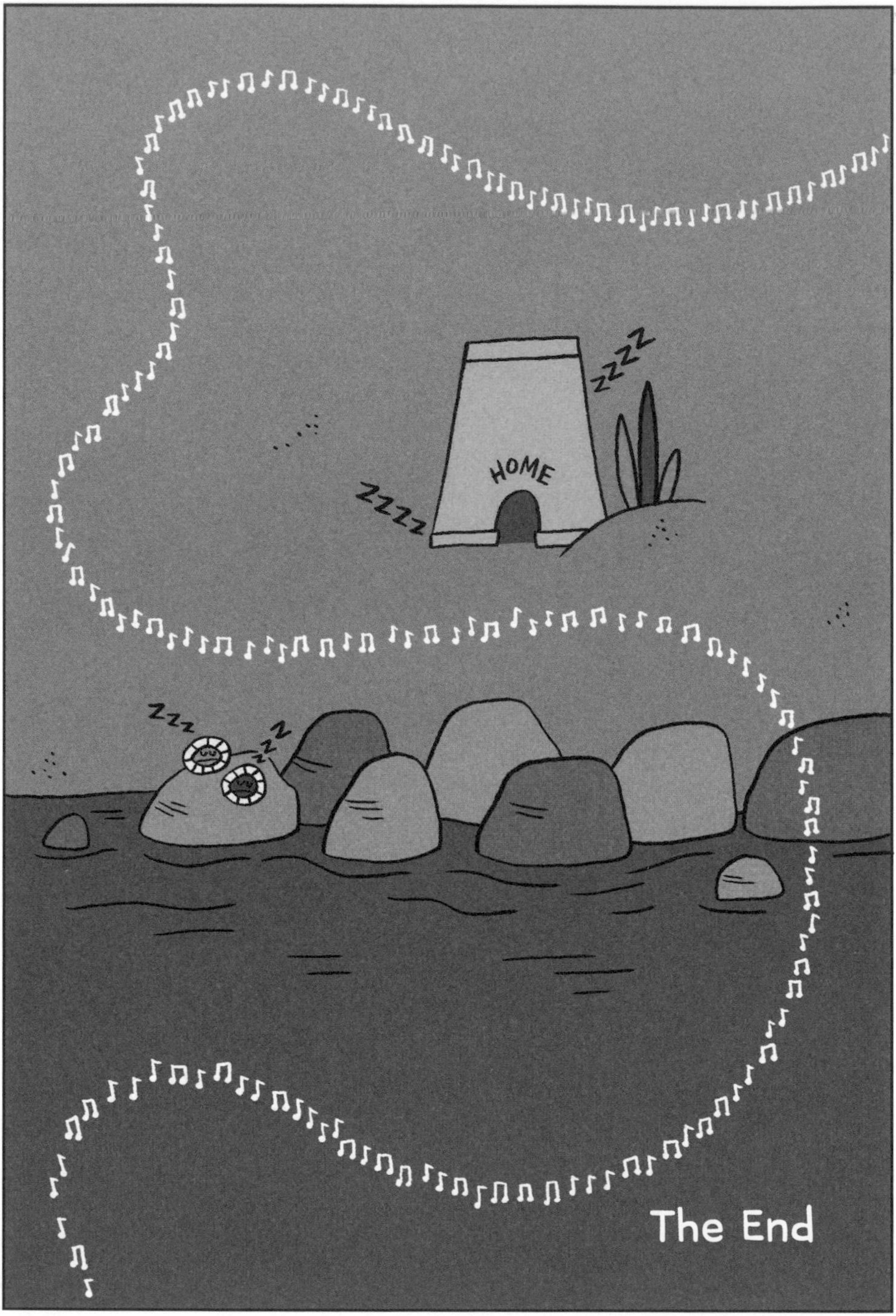
ZZZZ
HOME
ZZZZ
Zzz
ZZZ
The End

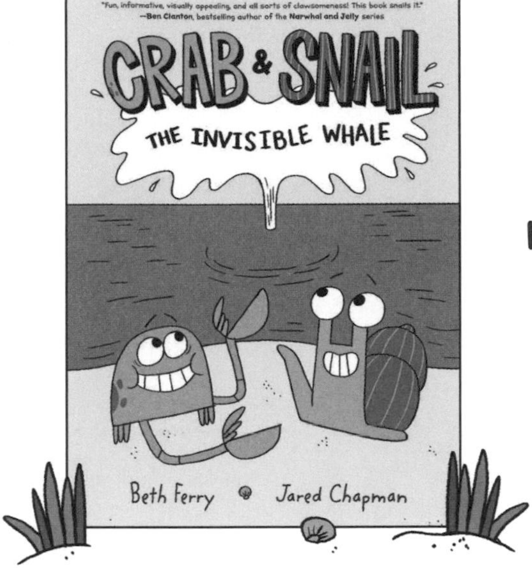
"Fun, informative, visually appealing, and all sorts of clawsomeness! This book snails it."
—Ben Clanton, bestselling author of the Narwhal and Jelly series
CRAB & SNAIL
THE INVISIBLE WHALE
Beth Ferry
Jared Chapman

Check out more seaside adventures!

And don't miss Crab and Snail's next adventure . . .

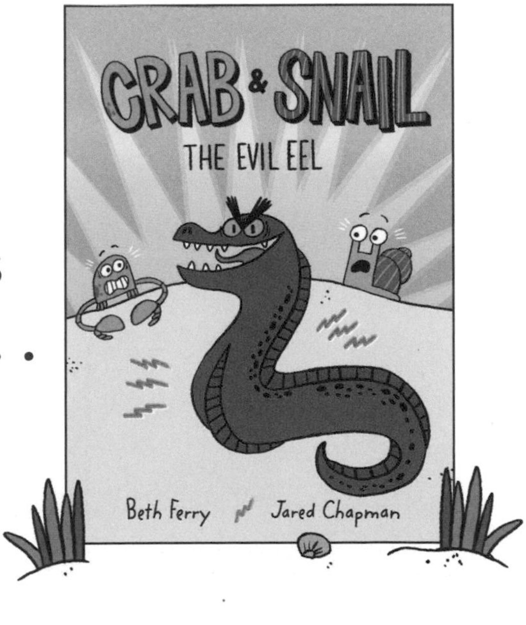
CRAB & SNAIL
THE EVIL EEL
Beth Ferry
Jared Chapman

Beth Ferry lives and writes by the beach in New Jersey where she has looked into many a tidal pool. She loves these tiny, salty puddles because they magically appear at low tide and always have the coolest things in them. Beth loves writing about the wonders of the beach and never fails to learn something new with every story she writes. You can learn something new about Beth at www.bethferry.com.

Jared Chapman is the author and illustrator of books such as *Vegetables in Underwear*, *T. Rex Time Machine*, and *Steve, Raised by Wolves*. When he isn't breaking trampolines and blaming it on invisible sea life, Jared lives with his wife and four kids in Northeast Texas. Visit him online at www.jaredchapman.com.